I smiled again, and when I did I saw the gratitude for it on his face—the stunned joy. He was really young. Straggly black hair. That wrinkled Sunday school T-shirt. He must have just gotten his license, if he even had it yet, and gone off for the afternoon in his mother's station wagon, looking for girls. And then, this jackpot, this peek into boy heaven.

He would never catch up, but I'd given him this glimpse of it, and he smiled back.

"So long, suckers!" Desiree yelled as we passed.

When I raised my hand from the steering wheel to wave, they were already gone.

I didn't look in my rearview mirror, but if I had, I would have seen only a radiant emptiness where they'd been.

Also by Laura Kasischke

Feathered

boy heaven

LAURA KASISCHKE

HARPER TEEN
An Imprint of HarperCollins*Publishers*

HarperTeen is an imprint of HarperCollins Publishers.

Boy Heaven

For information address HarperCollins Children's Books, a division of HarperCollins Publishers, 1350 Avenue of the Americas, New York, NY 10019.
www.harperteen.com

Library of Congress Cataloging-in-Publication Data
Kasischke, Laura, 1961–
Boy heaven / Laura Kasischke.— 1st ed.
p. cm.
Summary: While attending cheerleading camp, seventeen-year-old Kristy Sweetland and two of her friends begin to have forebodings after an encounter with three teenaged boys.
ISBN 978-0-06-081316-1
[1. Camps—Fiction. 2. Ghosts—Fiction. 3. Cheerleading—Fiction.] I. Title.
PZ7.K1178Boy 2006 2005017664
[Fic]—dc22 CIP
AC

Typography by Andrea Vandergrift

First HarperTeen paperback edition, 2008

For Bill

Every year, there were stories told around the campfire. At the center of it, a thin branch always blazed with a thousand pine needles, which turned red, then exploded, one by one—each a quick hiss followed by shriveling.

The spicy smell of white pine drifted out of the darkness of the national forest. Bug spray. Damp moss. The gooey blackened melodrama of roasted marshmallows.

A handful of bats slapped across a dark-blue sky. The sky was punctured with stars.

Year after year, the stories were the same—gruesome and spooky and *true*—and a few of the girls kept their hands over their faces during the telling:

First, there was the babysitter who went upstairs late one night because she thought she heard the children jumping on their beds and found them instead in the bathtub with their throats slashed.

Then there was the mother who got a phone call from her daughter. "Mama, I'm burning," the daughter sobbed. The mother screamed, but the line went dead, and a few seconds later a police officer rang the doorbell and said, "Ma'am, I'm sorry to have to tell you that your daughter was killed in a bus crash on her way home from school today."

There was the girl who was dared at a slumber party to write a love note to Satan, sign it in blood, and burn it—she thought it was funny—and who was found in the morning naked, hanging from a jump rope in the garage.

The ghost of a French explorer who creeps up behind campers in the Blanc Couer National Forest when they wander off the path to pee. And the little boy who fell out of a tall pine and broke his neck and now amuses himself by pushing people out of trees. The man who tied heavy chains around the body of his wife after he killed her, tossed the body off a bridge into Lake Michigan, then came home and found her sitting in his La-Z-Boy—smiling, soaking wet.

And this:

A girl who, with two friends, sneaked out of Pine Ridge Cheerleading Camp in a little red sports car one summer afternoon, and smiled at a couple of boys in a rusty station wagon....

One

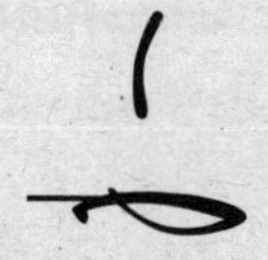

The red Mustang, like a small shiny thought dipped in blood, sped between two walls of white pine that extended as far ahead as the eye could see and as far behind as the rearview mirror could contain.

I was the driver.

The little car was mine.

My name was Kristy Sweetland, I was seventeen, and it felt as if someone had cut this particular path out of the Blanc Coeur National Forest for me—a narrow winding river of tar so smooth, my tires traveling over it sounded like nothing but breath and kisses, kisses and breath.

The top was down. The stereo was on. Beside me, my best friend, Desiree, had her ankles crossed on the dashboard, her polished legs shining in the sun. Behind us, a girl from camp whose name was also Kristi (although hers ended in an i), was holding onto her red hair, making noises.

"Come *on,*" she said, not for the first time. "This is ridiculous. Let's pull over and put the top up."

But Desiree and I didn't want to put the top up.

It was a perfect day to drive with it down.

The sky was clean and blue and crossed with frothy jet trails and meandering clouds. As we drove, the breeze made a smothering *whoosh* around us, and the air smelled like a Pink Pearl eraser I used to keep on my desk in elementary school—immaculate (I used to hold that eraser to my nose when I was bored, breathe in the dense pink dust, which had rubbed away hundreds of my mistakes and still smelled clean). It was fun, driving on a day like that, slicing straight through the nothing, turning it into wind.

My car was fast and flashy. It had a white vinyl interior and a silver horse on the hood. Beside me, Desiree was casual and gorgeous, and when we passed other cars, the drivers, who'd caught a glimpse of her out of the corner of their eyes, would snap their heads around to look at her again.

I was also young and pretty, beside her, behind the wheel of my red car, and I knew it. They looked at me, too, when they were done looking at her.

I wasn't beautiful, the way she was (I knew that, too), or dazzling like the other Kristi in my backseat, with her red hair and black-lashed green eyes—but I had what I wanted out of life for the moment: long hair, big blue eyes, rosy cheeks, a good tan, a white smile, big-enough breasts, and a little red convertible.

Desiree and I had been best friends since kindergarten. Inseparable. At school, in the hallways, the other kids looked nervous when we laughed. They didn't want to be laughed at by us.

It felt powerful, being pretty—but I also wanted to be good. I believed in God. And in Jesus. And in "Pretty is as pretty does," which my stepfather used to say whenever I stood in front of the mirror too long.

I didn't know what it meant, exactly. Could pretty *do* anything? It wasn't a verb, I knew that much. Under some circumstances I supposed it could be a noun. But I tried to be humble, and nice, anyway. I wasn't like Desiree, with a handful of snow for a heart. (Once she'd stuffed a gum wrapper into the Salvation Army bucket outside the mall, pretending it was a dollar, and when the bellringer had said, "Thank you, miss! God bless you!" Desiree replied, "God bless you, too," with such sincerity I couldn't help laughing, although I also knew I could never have done a thing like that.) But I supposed it was possible that if I'd been beautiful, like her, instead of just pretty, like me, I might not have been so humble.

But I got popular because of it.

Voted this, voted that, voted everything.

It was a bounty, what came along with being friendly and pretty at the same time. No one expected it. If you could do it and make it look sincere—be nice to the ugly girls, smile at the losers and the geeks, talk to them in the cafeteria as if they were normal people, invite a few of them to your parties even though your friends would stick their fingers down their throats and pretend to gag when you read the invitation list—the rewards were endless.

"Miss Congeniality," the assistant principal called me when he passed me in the hallway. "A smile for everyone," he said, and I'd smile.

And I got good grades, not because I was so smart, but because I studied hard and paid attention in class. I could carry a tune, sort of, and was elected president of the choir.

Once, in homeroom, I slipped into my seat, coming in late after a student council meeting, and Brad Bain, who sat behind me, said something to me I'd never forget.

Brad Bain was adopted, and everyone knew it because his brothers were tall and blond and athletic and he was short and dark-haired and pigeon-toed.

After I shoved my books under my desk, he leaned over and said to me in a whisper, "How'd you get so perfect?"

I looked at him—really looked at him for the first time—and saw myself reflected in his glasses, which were flecked with the skin that shed from his forehead and scalp, and I realized that he wasn't being sarcastic or even complimenting me. He simply wanted to know.

"Look," the red-headed Kristi in the backseat called up to us. "*Pull over*. I've *had* it."

Desiree looked at me, rolled her eyes, but I nodded into the rearview mirror at this Kristi, whose mirrored sunglasses reflected mine reflecting hers reflecting mine. (A dizzying riddle: If it hadn't been so pointless, we could have looked into each other's faces for an eternity and seen nothing but ourselves.) Kristi's voice had a tone that made it sound as if she'd been telling people all her life what to do, and they'd been doing it.

It was a tone that made Desiree want to kill her, I knew, but made me want to do what she said. It seemed as though it would be much less trouble to keep her happy than it would be to deal with the aftermath of making her mad. We'd only known her for two days, and she looked flammable—all that red hair, the pale skin, the improbably green eyes. Looking at her in my rearview mirror, I remembered how once, when I was a little girl playing in the backyard, a can of paint thinner had exploded on the neighbors' patio.

It spilled flames all over, and my stepfather aimed the garden hose at it until it sizzled out. It had simply been left in the sun too long, I was told. A few days later I found a bit of blackened paper in my sandbox that had drifted over into our yard. The part that wasn't burned away said, *anger: Haz—*

It took years before I'd understand that the word on that label had been *danger,* not *anger.*

I glanced at Desiree. We needed gas anyway. And candy. Cigarettes? Soda? "Okay, okay," I said, and made a fast left into a gas station, which had appeared so suddenly at the side of the road I almost missed it.

"Whoa," Desiree said, holding onto the dashboard and leaning into my shoulder as I turned. "Some warning next time, Speedy?"

A muffled bell rang as I ran over the black hose that was stretched between gas pumps. As we rolled to a stop (the wind suddenly dead, the stereo too loud, the earth seeming to have quit turning so abruptly we almost lurched off—our hair a mess, the clouds frozen in the sky), an old man materialized out of the glare of glass and cinder block and asked, "Fill 'er up?"

"Yes," I said, snapping the stereo off, still catching my breath, "please."

It was always like that, stopping after driving fast in my convertible. There was a moment when it was embarrassing: *Oh.* Flushed and winded, hair wild, sometimes still shouting, having not yet noticed that you no longer needed to scream to be heard—abruptly returned to the regular world.

The old man was wearing a navy blue jumpsuit with the name "Lute" embroidered on the pocket. In the backseat, the redhead was pawing at her hair, trying to put it back where she wanted it, and Lute, unscrewing my gas cap, said to her sympathetically, "You can buy yourself a little comb in there, sweetheart," nodding at the station.

"I've got one in my pocket," the redhead told him, "but it'll just rip my hair out now, with all these tangles."

"Holy cripes," Lute said. "Don't do that."

I set my sunglasses on the dashboard, opened the car door, and stepped out.

Without the sunglasses, the chrome dazzle of the gas station parking lot was blinding. I had to shield my eyes with my hand. The only thing I could look at directly was the parking lot, its black tar gone soft in the heat. On its surface, several small black pools of oil swirled with pastel scarves, and the shadow of my body cast itself over those shadows.

Overhead, there was a long, sharp cicada chirr. It paused and surged, surged and paused, sounding as if it were coming from the phone lines—frenzied, electrical, a thousand hysterical mothers chattering in the sky.

Across the lot at the air pump was a yellow bus with CHRIST IS KING painted on its side in black letters. A bald man was kneeling at its left tire—filling it, or praying to it. The bus had been left running, and to pass it I had to walk through a dieseled curtain of exhaust. I held my breath inside that curtain, but the smell entered me anyway, along with a seamless memory of every bus ride I'd ever taken—buses to school, to games, to camps—miles and miles of vibration between where I'd started and where I was going.

In the plate-glass window of the gas station, wavering through that film of fumes, I could see my reflection—an image of myself layered over with baby blue stenciled letters:

MARLBORO/carton/5.45

How old was that sign?

In that glass, I was see-through, and floating

around inside my body were gas pumps, an ice machine, and a few cans of Valvoline.

Still, my reflection was solid enough that I could see myself—my hair a dark mess, my halter top white as a sail. I could also see that the man who'd been kneeling at the bus tire had stood up, still holding his hissing air hose, to watch me walk across the parking lot, and another man, just done rearranging some bags of cedar chips in the back of his pickup, also watched me as he lit a cigarette.

Through my transparent shoulder I saw the brief gem of his Bic make a stab at the air, while all around me the metallic buzz of cicadas droned, the electric knife of their whining sliding around my flesh.

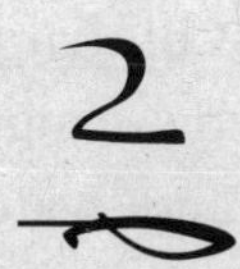

It had only begun that morning—the sound of those cicadas, which was everywhere now, taking up all the space of the silence I hadn't even noticed before.

That morning, just before sunrise, I'd woken to the first voiceless whining, only inches from my face, and I'd sat up fast, shaking out my hair, feeling the sound before I heard it—feeling it in my *hair.*

The cabin was cold and dewy, dappled with early morning sun shining weakly through the trees, and it smelled of shampooed hair—yards and yards of it, enough strawberry-scented hair to fill a hundred bushel baskets. That screaming thing, whatever it was, was not in my hair, or inside my head, or on my pillow, but was clinging to the window screen, scanning the cabin with its weird mechanical eyes, its round mouth-hole buzzing *oooh-aaah, oooh-aaah.*

The utter ugliness of that thing so close to my face shocked me, and I caught my breath, put a hand to my chest, and watched, trying not to move.

It was no longer than a finger, but it had wide, red-veined wings and those nasty claws with which it clung to the screen. Its awful iridescent eyes, searching, seemed to freeze when they met mine, and then it flew backward in a blur of sound and was gone.

And then the sound was picked up by the whole sky.

An oscillating chirr. A magnetic screaming muffled by metal, sounding as if someone had opened Pandora's box, then nailed it shut before anything could get out.

But what was in there definitely *wanted* out, and the full horror of it struck me then—that there were hundreds, *thousands,* of those things out there. "Oh my God," I said, more loudly than I'd meant to say it.

The red-haired Kristi, who slept in the cot beside mine, rolled over then and blinked. "Was that a mosquito?" she asked.

"No," I answered. "Definitely not."

Her eyes were open now—green and white and bloodshot. Although I'd only met her two days before, already I'd grown used to the shallow, intimate whisper of this Kristi's breath as she slept.

Asleep, she was a rhythm, a sibilance, like her name, *Kristi Smith*—an hourglass filled with sand being turned over and over from one end of the night to the other. But, awake, she was one long complaint. In only the first few minutes of our acquaintance she'd told me that she hadn't wanted to come to cheerleading camp, that she was thoroughly exasperated to be spending a week away from Crystal River and her boyfriend and her swim club there, that she didn't like the forest, that she couldn't eat the food in the dining hall, that she'd heard there were leeches in all the lakes, and that she was going to refuse to swim—but, also, that she was thc captain of hcr squad, a position for which another girl in Crystal River would be chosen if she had refused to attend cheerleading camp that summer.

When I told her that I, myself, had come to Pine Ridge Cheerleading Camp every summer for the last four years and that it was really a lot of fun, she rolled her eyes.

About the insect, she asked, "Well, what was it then?"

"I don't know," I answered.

"A cicada," our counselor asserted cheerfully from her cot—the cot closest to the door, situated there to discourage girls from trying to sneak out of the cabin in the night. She propped herself up on her elbows to tell us, "It's their seventeenth year."

Amanda. "Mandy," she'd said, introducing herself over tepid hamburgers in the dining hall on the first night.

She was a college cheerleader, a girl with legs that looked as if they'd been buffed and shined by a machine but who, when she wasn't cartwheeling or doing the splits or brushing her ash-brown hair in front of the bathroom mirror, wore a pair of wire-rimmed glasses and seemed proud to be full of college-level knowledge and advice.

Already she'd announced to a g[illegible] leaders in the bathroom that it was c[illegible] know never to put Vaseline in our va[illegible]

She'd reached into a girl's make[illegible] snatched out a small jar of it, held it up [illegible] one to see—smokily yellow, the content[illegible]ining dully, looking like a tablespoon of fat—and explained that it was a little known fact that the vagina was completely unequipped to rid itself of petroleum jelly, *ever*.

"Jesus Christ," Desiree had said as we walked together out the bathroom door. "What made her think we were planning to put Vaseline in our vaginas?"

"Really," I agreed. "And how does she know that once it gets up there it's up there for good?"

After that, Desiree nicknamed Mandy Slippery Lips.

Slippery Lips swung her legs out of her sleeping bag and began a little lecture on cicadas.

"It's their seventeenth year," she repeated. "For seventeen years they've been underground, waiting to come up. To mate. In another day or two, they'll be gone."

In response to this information there was the deep, silent apathy of dreaming cheerleaders. Their pale palms dangled off the sides of their cots. I imagined dust settling there all night, each girl waking up with a free handful of starry ash.

They were strangers to me, and I could remember only a few of their names. The Kristi beside me. The tall girl, Rebecca. The one with the scar under her nose, Michelle. The rest were a blur of Saras and Beths. We'd already spent two nights only inches from one another's most vulnerable selves—dreaming, muttering, drooling into small cold pillows—but we were complete strangers to one another. It was the policy of Pine Ridge Cheerleading Camp to split girls from the same schools up for cabin assignments so new friendships could be formed, old cliques discouraged. Although Desiree was two cabins away, she might as well have been on another continent. There wasn't even a path from my cabin to hers. All paths from the cabins led to the bathroom or to the dining hall, nowhere else.

So far, I was the only one who'd actually seen the cicada itself, although the noise of it had already slipped completely over the cabin like a frantic shroud, and I couldn't help being curious. *I* was seventeen as well.

"Where do they go?" I asked, trying to picture it, trying to imagine what kind of nest or cave or hive was waiting for those things to return to it after they'd mated. I pictured a white funnel, something made out of paper, glue, cellophane—the kind of thing a little girl might make in art class out of papier-mâché and an empty milk carton, but *huge.*

"They die," Slippery Lips said, still smiling.

The noise of the cicadas seemed to swell outside the cabin in response to this answer—*yeah, yeah, yeah*—sounding magnetic, exploratory, edged with death.

"They mate," she said, "then lay eggs, then die, and the cycle starts again. It's the males that make the noise."

Beside me, the red-haired Kristi was lying on her side, looking over at Slippery Lips with an expression of sleepy and skeptical repulsion—eyes narrowed, mouth open, as if cicadas were the last straw. She huffed in annoyance when I asked another question.

"What did they do underground for seventeen years?"

I simply wanted to know—but it was a habit, asking questions, that often caused my classmates and squadmates to sigh and roll their eyes. Once, in World Religions, I'd raised my hand to ask Mr. Yarbrough if he thought God might be a woman, and Matt Reed, who sat behind me, grabbed my hand in midair and whispered into my neck, "For God's sake don't encourage the man. You're always egging him on." A whispered chorus of *yeah*s came from every corner of the classroom then, and I never asked my question.

"They ate tree roots," Slippery Lips said, shrugging, "and grew wings. You know, got stronger. Got ready."

"God," the red-haired Kristi said. She rolled over onto her other side. "Gross me out completely."

"It's not gross," Slippery Lips said defensively, as if cicadas had been her idea. "It's *nature.*"

And she was right, of course; it *was* nature. But I also had to admit that the red-haired Kristi was right too. It was gross.

As I lay on my cot next to hers, listening to the racket those things were making overhead, imagining them—the millions of them, red-eyed in the pines, with those veins in their wings and the small dark holes of their mouths busy shaping the dentist-drill sound of a scream, I could see why she'd rolled over, refused to hear any more.

It was a cheerleader's nightmare—a swarm of screaming bugs hovering over cheerleading camp all week.

Still, I wanted to believe that I wasn't really like this other Kristi, either, with her allergies and phobias, her pale skin and little cotton balls soaked in face toner, which she dabbed over her forehead and around her nose every few hours so she wouldn't get oily. On the windowsill over her cot she kept a huge bottle of Phisoderm, and in the back pocket of her shorts she carried a big-handled pink plastic comb and pulled it out every few minutes to fluff up, or smooth down, her hair.

Already, Desiree had nicknamed her Little Miss Frigid because, during a discussion the first night in the bathroom about the camp director and whether or not the enormity of his hands and feet might be an indication of the size of his penis, the redhead had shaken her head and said, "I can't *believe* this," packing up her toothbrush and hurrying out. We'd all burst out laughing as soon as the door closed behind her.

Still, in truth, none of us was really that different from her, and we knew it. Like her, we'd all spend much of the morning in the bathroom blow-drying our hair just to go swimming that afternoon. And we'd squeal and scatter when some girl on the trail stepped on a slug with her flip-flop and had to scrape it off with a stick.

There were *plenty* of things about the natural world that I myself found so gross I couldn't stand to hear about them.

Snakes. Vomit. Death. The soft awful phlegm inside the shell of a snail—the part that was the snail.

Like all the girls I knew, I was squeamish. I'd done badly in biology class the year before because I hadn't been able to look inside the body cavity of my dissected fetal pig—its pink skin peeled back, smelling of babies and ham and my mother's White Shoulders perfume—and catalog its organs.

Its moist infant eyelids were closed, but I still had the feeling that it was watching me, that it could sense the violation of my fingertips inside its little cave, that its tender flesh recoiled each time the silver tweezers passed over its body.

Mr. Nestor sighed when I told him softly that

I was worried I might faint. He checked a box, told me to put my pig away, and that was the end of that semester of the marking period.

But then, in the spring, we were assigned to make an insect collection, required to gather at least ten different specimens, and label and mount them. We were each given a jar and a small sponge soaked in chloroform—a little pad of lethal cologne—and sent into the field behind the baseball diamond.

Right away, I caught a grasshopper—an ugly, army green thing that spewed something brown all over the inside of my jar and then fell onto its back, wagging its legs in a slow dance on the chloroformed pad. Without thinking, I tossed the whole thing, jar and all, into some weeds and walked away.

I didn't feel sorry for the grasshopper, or particularly guilty. I'd stepped on hundreds of bugs in my life. Swatted them. Squished them. Flushed them down the toilet.

But this one—its death was so *incomplete.* I felt afraid that it might have some new surprise in store for me before it was over. That it would make a noise, or bloom into some extra awfulness.

Explode. Call my name. I just wanted to be rid of it. Immediately. The field beyond the baseball diamond was stony and dry, and under the parched grass it was all gravel and sand glittering like glass, and when I sat down, the sharp stubble of it scratched my thighs. I was wearing my cheerleading skirt and bobby socks because it was Spirit Day, and later there'd be an assembly where our squad would scream at the student body, "We've got spirit, yes we do! We've got spirit, how 'bout you?" and they would scream the same thing back at us.

When I looked up, I saw Bob Larson slouching toward me in his baggy overalls, already bearing a jarful of moths and butterflies flapping their wings slowly, as though against great wind, and bumping groggily against the glass. He had a grasshopper too, identical to the one I'd abandoned, and his was also lying on its back, pedaling its legs in slow motion over its body.

I knew Bob Larson liked me. For years he'd been glancing in my direction whenever he had the chance—study hall, cafeteria, lull in a class discussion. But this was the first time he'd ever walked straight over to me, smiling. I looked up at him and said, "I'm going to flunk this project."

"Oh no you're not," he said.

When Bob Larson had finished it, my project was perfect:

Ten dry and unbroken specimens pinned to a piece of Styrofoam that had been cut to fit the bottom of a cigar box. He presented it to me at my locker the Monday morning it was due. When he put it in my hands, for a moment I was completely unable to speak.

It was so beautiful.

The moth had its wings spread as if in flight, and I'd never seen anything so delicate in my life. Inside those papery fans there were threadlike white veins through which, I imagined, blood made out of air, or imagination, flowed. Its body was like a thread, but dusted with chalk, or some substance that shimmered pinkly in the fluorescent light of the high school hallway. Looking at it, I wondered why, the week before, out past the baseball diamond with the mason jar, I'd been so afraid. Now, these insects looked like baubles, decorations, bits of frill I'd have been perfectly happy to wear in my hair. Even the grasshopper looked harmless and happy. Jaunty. A little arrogant, with his wings folded behind him and his nasty little head held high.

Pinned to Styrofoam by Bob Larson in the bottom of a cigar box, these insects did not look *dead,* because they did not appear to have ever been alive.

"Like it?" he asked.

"*Love* it," I said, and hugged him in the hallway.

And although I was grateful to him, I never went out with him. He never asked, and for this I was also grateful since, if he had, because of the insect collection and because I'd just broken up with Chip again and everyone knew I didn't have another boyfriend yet, I'd have had to go.

"Maybe he's one of those guys who'd rather just watch from a distance," Desiree had suggested.

Desiree deeply believed she knew everything there was to know about boys and was quick to sort them according to categories:

Guys Who'd Rather Just Watch from a Distance. Guys Who Want a Girl to Pretend They Don't Exist. Guys Who Like Cars More Than They Like Girls.

But there was something else about Bob Larson—something larger and more generous, stranger and more dangerous and even more appealing than Desiree's explanation seemed able to capture. I liked to think of him as removed from such mundane things. When I thought of Bob Larson I always pictured him sheathed in glassy light, smiling sleepily, as if he were completely content on the other side of that glass, looking out.

3

When the glass door of the gas station had closed behind me, the sudden absence of cicada drone was deafening. And now that the sun was out of my eyes, I was blinded as well. I blinked, squinted, pushed the bangs away from my forehead and saw straps and daggers of light hanging in the air in front of me. I rubbed my eyes until I was able to look up again and scan the walls of the gas station for the candy display.

The Pay Days were four rows from the bottom, right next to the Mars bars.

Back at camp, I already had a duffel bag full of Pay Days, but it was the only kind of candy I liked, and I was hungry—a prickly fist inside my stomach. I hadn't eaten breakfast, and we'd sneaked out of camp before lunch, so I carried the candy bar, satisfyingly heavy in its white plastic wrapper, to the cash register and put it down on the counter.

"That it?" the guy at the register asked.

"Yes," I said.

He was tall, in his twenties I supposed. Pale hair and freckles. His hands were dirty, especially the fingernails, which were rimmed with black—and in the center of a gleaming white smile, he had one gray tooth.

I dug down into the pocket of my cutoffs for the coins.

"Where you going?" he asked.

"Lovers' Lake," I said.

"Where from?"

"Pine Ridge."

"The cheerleading camp?" he asked, raising an eyebrow.

"Uh-huh," I said.

Still smiling, he tossed the coins I'd given him into the register.

That tooth—it was exactly the color of a smudged dime.

"Have a great time," he said to my back as the bells on the door jangled and I stepped back into the glare and shifting fumes of the gas station parking lot, back into the high-voltage buzzing of cicadas.

The man who'd been kneeling at the bus wheel was kicking it now, and the smell of the parking lot was flowery and poisonous at the same time. The afternoon, which was warm but not too hot, managed somehow to be full of birdsong inserted into the gaps between motors growling and that cicada whine.

It was a perfect summer day.

A few children had wandered off the idling CHRIST IS KING bus, and they sat with their backs to the gas station in the shade. The pickup driver took a long last drag on his cigarette, then threw the butt of it over the children's heads into a grassy stretch between the parking lot and the road.

I leaned over the side of my car to get my purse and fished out the money I owed for the gasoline to Lute, who'd pumped it.

"Thank you," he said, taking the felty and worn-out bills, and smiling.

But he wasn't smiling at me.

He was smiling past me, at Desiree, who was

still in the car with her legs propped up on the dashboard and her mirrored sunglasses reflecting mostly blue and green, as if she were looking down at the world from space. She waved her fingers at Lute and smiled back.

The top was still down, and the white vinyl interior of my Mustang shone with brilliant softness. From the sky, my little red convertible would look like a lipsticked smile, I thought—and at the center of that smile, was Desiree, lounging in an orange tube top and white satin shorts (through which her bikini underpants with their little smiley faces were clearly visible, and which showed a good two inches of her pale butt cheeks when she bent over). Her sandals had slipped off. Her toenails were hot pink. She said, "I talked Little Miss Frigid out of it. I gave her a bandana to put on her head and told her we'd be at the lake in a few minutes anyway and that we were *not* going to put the top up."

"Where is she now?" I asked.

"Went to the bathroom to put on the bandana."

I leaned against the warm hood of my car and

unwrapped the candy bar. Arrows of light stabbed up from the bumpers on the other cars, and my eyes watered from the brilliance, turning the whole scene into a smear of melted color and shape, as if the gas station and the CHRIST IS KING school bus, the gas pumps and the blacktop, had all been spilled around me out of a pitcher. I felt as if, at the center of it, I was being watched—the sense that eyes were on me, but when I looked around, I saw no one.

Salt and caramel stuck to my fingertips, which I licked.

It made me hungry, being at camp. Much hungrier than I ever felt at home where, night after night, my mother would set something steaming at the center of the dining room table. "Seconds anyone?" she'd ask, but I almost never asked for seconds.

But, every summer at Pine Ridge Cheerleading Camp, I was ravenous. I could have eaten seconds, thirds, fourths of anything my mother could have dished up. The year before, I'd eaten so much during the week of cheerleading camp that Desiree had started calling me the Burger Queen.

This year, as she and I rolled backward down my driveway in East Grand Rapids, my car trunk stuffed with our sleeping bags and duffel bags, my stepfather had called out, "Don't get eaten by a bear!" and Desiree had said, nudging me, "More like don't *eat* a bear."

It was an appetite that seemed to me to be fueled by the smell of pine needles, wood smoke, and the suggestion that, in the national forest, you were always at the edge of a big emptiness and that, if you stumbled off the path and got lost, you were going to need to have eaten enough at your last meal to last a long time.

When the other Kristi came out of the bathroom, her red hair was tucked under the blue bandana. A neon-pink bikini top blazed through her white T-shirt. She called over to us sullenly, "I'm going inside for something to drink."

"Get me something, too," Desiree called back.

"Me, too," I said, through my mouthful of candy.

She didn't say anything, just disappeared in the gas station glare.

"Do you think she'll do it?" Desiree asked.

"No," I answered.

The bus driver blew a whistle and the little kids in the grass stood up and began to file back onto the CHRIST IS KING bus. Their short legs barely seemed able to climb the black rubber steps, and I suddenly felt sorry for them, and looked away. It was too easy to imagine their homesickness and how it would hit them in nauseating waves as that bus rolled away from the station, taking them closer to whatever church camp they were going to, and farther from home.

The Blanc Coeur National Forest was full of camps like that. I'd gone to one myself, when I was ten—a Lutheran camp called Michi-Wa-Ka. But after only three nights there, I called my mother and begged her to pick me up, and she and my stepfather drove the four hours north without stopping until they'd pulled into the parking lot and found me at the Welcome Cabin, waiting with my sleeping bag to be taken home.

Another girl, an older girl, had told me in a whisper across our cots in the night that *Michi-Wa-Ka* was Indian for "Two Drowned Girls"--that the camp was haunted by the ghosts of two campers who'd tipped their canoe in the lake and never been found.

"If you get up in the middle of the night to go to the bathroom," she said, "you'll hear them crying for their mothers in the woods."

I lay awake for a long time after that, willing myself to sleep, willing myself not to see their blue faces and weedy hair rising to the surface of the lake, wide-eyed. And also willing myself not to need to pee. The girls' room was at the bottom of a little hill from our cabin, and the path to it was surrounded by forest on every side.

Eventually, I did fall asleep, but when I woke up, my bladder was burning and my heart was pounding, and I knew it was either walk to the girls' room or wet the bed. I started to cry when I realized the hopelessness of the situation, and set my bare feet down sadly on the wooden floor. I wasn't five feet down the dirt path in my bare feet when I heard them.

It was a cold high plea, less like human voices than two terrible grief-stricken teapots screaming out of the ground. I peed in my nightgown and ran back to the cabin and into my cot and didn't move again until sunrise.

My mother never suggested camp again after that, and I'd never again asked to go until I was in junior high and went to Pine Ridge with Desiree. By then, I'd grown to believe that the sound I'd heard in the forest that night had come from my imagination.

The other Kristi came out of the Standard Station with three bottles of diet soda held by their necks in her hands. Her pale skin glowed against the plate glass behind her so that she looked like a girl being stalked by her own ghost. "Wow," I said in Desiree's direction. "She did it."

"I still hate her," Desiree whispered under her breath before smiling up at her as she handed the two bottles over to me. I passed one to Desiree, and she said, "Thanks!" in a tone so bright and false I almost laughed out loud. Instead, I turned my back quickly, twisted the cap off the bottle, and tossed it into the trashcan. The can was lined with a black plastic bag, and the sweetly sickening smell of something freshly dead rose out of it.

I sat down and put the bottle between my bare knees, where the cold burned against my skin. Beside me, Desiree smacked a cigarette out of her pack and said, "Want one?"

"No," I said, but she'd already put the pack back under the front seat of the car, knowing I wouldn't want one because I almost never smoked. And even when I did, it wasn't really smoking—not the way Desiree did it, the smoke disappearing inside her, coming back out in swirling scarves. Instead, I just let the smoke smear over my mouth, because on the few occasions I'd inhaled, I'd coughed so long and hard afterward that I thought I was going to throw up. The one time I'd smoked pot at a slumber party—my friends in their flannel nightgowns coaching, sitting around me in a circle, urging me to inhale—I actually did throw up.

Desiree lit her cigarette with a lighter she'd borrowed—or stolen—from her father's girlfriend. It was silver and engraved with an *A*, and although it opened and closed with an efficient little click, it always took her several tries to get it to light—beginning with a phantom flame, a slick gray shadow that smelled of butane.

"Let's just go back to camp," the Kristi in the

backseat said. I'd almost forgotten she was there.

"What?" Desiree said, whipping around with her mouth wide open to look at her. "*You* were the one who wanted to sneak out."

"So?" she answered.

I said, trying for a conciliatory tone, "I thought we were going swimming at Lovers' Lake," and looked at her through my rearview mirror. In that reflection she looked small and freckled.

"I never said I wanted to go to the lake," she said. "In fact, I said I *didn't* want to go to the lake. It's supposed to have leeches in it. All the lakes around here do."

"Oh bullshit," Desiree said. "I've been swimming in plenty of lakes up here, and I've never seen a fucking leech. If you don't want to swim you can sunbathe."

"I don't *sunbathe*," she said. "I'm a *redhead.*"

"Come on. This is the deepest lake in the state. It'll be cool. And it *was* your idea to sneak out of camp," I added—but carefully, watching the rearview mirror to gauge her expression. "We'd be at lunch now if you hadn't said you wanted to get out."

"*Really*," Desiree said.

And it *had* been her idea.

We'd been sitting in the bleachers for pep, and one of the coaches was shouting at us about school spirit through a megaphone:

"Cheerleading is teamwork! Cheerleading is hard work! Cheerleading is self-discipline and energy and personality and poise! It's sportsmanship and leadership and being in top physical condition! It's being proud of your*self* and your *school*! It's being the *best girl you can be*! Do *you* have what it takes?!"

"Yes!"

But the *yes* that rose up from the bleachers had sounded hushed against the louder whining of the cicadas, which seemed to have congregated in the pines directly over our heads. There were twenty-seven of us, but, screaming, we just sounded silly and weak against their *thousands* in the trees. The coach's jaw dropped, her eyes narrowed. She put her hands on her hips and shook her head, disapproval radiating out of her as if she, like the moon, were reflecting some greater source of disapproval burning out there in heaven.

She was pregnant, and her long, white-blond hair was gathered in a ribboned ponytail, which she'd tossed over her right shoulder.

Behind her, the thin pines shivered, and the sun on them made it look as if each needle on each tree had been coated with some kind of slippery substance—butter, spit, Vaseline—so that the shining was both brilliant and smudged. The sky was so blue, it looked painted. The few wispy clouds that lay flat above the pines did not look like clouds. They looked like cotton, or an artist's rendering of clouds in which the clouds had been made to look like cotton.

"I didn't *hear* you!" the pep coach shouted, sounding furious.

We shouted back, *"Yes!"*

This time there was, perhaps, more emphasis on the *s*—but it only made the *yes-s-s* sound like hissing and impatience, and she turned her face away from it as if we'd spat at her. She began tapping the toe of her white canvas shoe at the woodchips beneath her, and then looked up and spat back, "Fine. Forget it. Instead of pep, we can do *sit-ups*. Maybe *tomorrow* morning you'll be a bit *peppier.*"

A groan rose from the bleachers.

A groan of infinite weariness.

A chain gang of cheerleaders in hell being told they'd be pushing a rock up the side of a hill for all of eternity.

It was then that the redhead had leaned over and said to me, "You've got a car, don't you?"

"Yeah."

"Let's get out of here," she said.

I turned to Desiree, who'd heard us.

In truth, I always looked to Desiree for the answer to questions like this: Should we? Now? Do we want to? *Should* we want to?

She was my best friend, and had been since kindergarten. She'd taught me to cartwheel. Cat's Cradle. Jump rope. The trick to removing the patient's heart during Operation so the buzzer didn't go off, the patient's red nose flashing to show you'd killed him. Once, she'd even saved my life. We were nine years old, playing hopscotch on the sidewalk in front of her house, when I accidentally inhaled a piece of cinnamon candy.

One minute, it was in my mouth, slipping over and under my tongue, turning into a glass arrowhead; and the next minute it was gone, and the world stopped turning. The *whole world* screeched to a halt, and when I opened my mouth and looked around, I saw the frozen shrubs, and the statue that had once been my best friend, and the way my shadow had dissolved on the sidewalk leaving a silver film in the shape of the girl I'd been, and when I opened my mouth wider to try to breathe, I realized that there was no longer any such thing as air. Although I was only nine years old, I understood at that moment that the world had been invented entirely by my breathing, and that now that I'd stopped breathing, the world was going to end.

Then, Desiree slapped me on the back, the candy flew from my mouth, the world was turning again, and Desiree laughed.

She was my best friend, but I was her *only* friend.

They hated her, other girls.

"Boy crazy" was the nice term for it, but someone had spray-painted the back of the concession stand at the football field last fall with DESIREE WILDER IS A NYMPHO. Even in elementary school.

One time, I went looking for Desiree at recess and found her in a concrete tunnel on our playground, sitting next to Scotty Schneider. It was winter, she had her plaid skirt pulled up, and

Scotty Schneider had put a handful of snow in Desiree's white underpants. Together they were just sitting and watching as it melted.

And then one Saturday night eight years later, Desiree called at ten o'clock while I was watching television with my mother, and she whispered ecstatically into the phone, "I did it."

"What?" I asked—not because I wondered what she'd done, but because I hadn't heard what she'd said.

"I had *sex,*" she said, "with Tony Sparrow."

I held more tightly to the phone receiver, all the breath so thoroughly knocked out of my body that I not only couldn't speak, I couldn't see. It appeared to me that the kitchen, where our phone was attached to the wall, had begun to melt—the refrigerator and the stove and the stools at the breakfast nook swirling and slopping in dull splashes onto the floor. We were in junior high. I had not yet been kissed, myself, by a boy, or held a boy's hand, or even been alone in a room with a boy I wasn't babysitting or who was not my cousin.

And then Desiree's mother died—a blood clot that worked its way straight to her heart one spring morning while she was pushing Desiree's little sister on a tire swing—and Tony Sparrow turned into Rob Manning, a much older boy who wanted Desiree to run away with him, and then into Mario Raymo, a Venezuelan exchange student. Then we started high school, and, ever since, Desiree had never had fewer than two boyfriends at a time—usually three, each of whom would be kept thoroughly oblivious to the others until some cataclysmic event at a football game or in the parking lot afterward, when all her deceptions would be exposed and she would have to start all over. Then, she'd be done for a while with the football stars and move on to the kinds of boys who played guitar in the talent show and sang like Neil Young.

And then the math whiz.

And then another exchange student—this time from Sri Lanka.

One night at a party, I overheard that boy telling a group of drunken jocks that back in Sri Lanka—a place none of us could ever have found on a map (was it an island?)—that he had a girlfriend he was going to marry. But when Desiree pulled him out behind the garage, he changed his mind, it seemed, about his whole life—and that week he wrote to the girlfriend and told her it was over, that he was in love with an American girl named Desiree.

And then Desiree told him she was sorry he'd taken things so seriously.

Maybe she'd laughed a little when she said this.

And then a few months after that, she told two different senior boys that she'd go with them to the prom, and then went with a third.

"Oh *please*," she'd said when Mary Beth Brummler, whose older brother had been one of the boys, told her after cheerleading practice that she was a bitch.

"How can you be friends with her?" I was asked in locker rooms, on buses, at parties, in the library standing in line to check out books. "You're so nice."

I'd smile and shrug. "So is she," I'd say, trying not to sound defensive. "Just in a different way."

"Well?"

The redhead was waiting for my answer—whether or not we'd be sneaking out of camp in my car.

"Dez?" I asked, and Desiree shrugged—a gesture she made at least ten times a day, a fluid *who-cares* that made it look as if there were weightless packages on her shoulders, slipping right off.

We dropped off the side of the bleachers when the other girls stood to position themselves on the wood chips for sit-ups, and then we ran for the woods and for the parking lot before anyone could see us leave.

"Well," Desiree said, turning around again to look at the red-haired Kristi. "*We're* going to Lovers' Lake. If *you* want to wait here, or walk back—"

"Okay, okay. Let's go to the lake."

I turned the key in the ignition, and my car made the sound I loved—a simple growl followed by purring—a sound that always reminded me how much I loved it. It had been a present the year before, for my sixteenth birthday. When I had come down to breakfast that morning, my stepfather had presented the keys to me wrapped up in pink tissue paper.

"A Mustang," he'd said, following me out the door to the garage. "It's used, but it belonged to a little old lady who only drove it to church on Sundays."

I let it purr for a moment at the gas pump, waiting while Lute walked in front of us, across the parking lot, in answer to the bell of a woman who'd driven up to one of the pumps in a blue Skylark with three children in her backseat.

I squinted behind my sunglasses to see them.

Those children looked sad back there—small and trapped and tired.

Then, when I checked the mirrors to see if it was safe to pull away from the pump, Desiree said, "Don't look at them."

"Those kids?" I asked, looking over at the Skylark again, into the backseat, where one of them was sucking its thumb.

"*No,*" Desiree said. "The losers."

"What losers?" I asked, looking around.

"Over there," she said, nodding to the spot where the CHRIST IS KING bus had been parked. Now, there was a rusty station wagon parked there instead.

Two boys inside it were staring in our direction.

5

I had seen a dead boy before.

Miles Kruger.

The only dead person I'd seen besides my grandmother.

It had been basketball season, an away game. *(Tonight is the night! The time is now! The Hornets are here to show you how!)* And it was a long bus ride to get there. To make the time go faster, one of the guys had brought hash brownies wrapped in tinfoil. Another had brought vodka mixed with Gatorade. Someone had snitched pills from his mother's medicine chest and was generously passing them out to his teammates.

The boys were drunk, or stoned, or both, and getting rowdy. But the cheerleaders, as always, were abstaining. We'd been coached more carefully in the EGR High School Athletic Code of Conduct, which contained a long statement forbidding drugs and alcohol, especially while in the school's athletic uniform.

"You girls," our coach, Margo, always told us seriously on the first day of the season, "have been chosen for this squad because you represent EGR High girls at their best. You are in *front* of the crowd for a reason, and you must never forget it. To stay in the *front*, you must live up to the *code*."

The boys?

They must have gotten a different talk about the code. A few true athletes sat up front behind the driver, staring straight ahead, preparing themselves for the game. They were respected, but had no nicknames, and their teammates never poured cans of beer over their heads at the end-of-season parties—although, without them, there would never have been a season.

It was winter.

On the other side of the bus' steamed windows, a deep blue slush was being dumped out of the sky. I wrote my name in loopy cursive in that steam. Some boy started to sing an obnoxious song. Another boy told him to shut up.

"*You* shut up!"

"*You* shut up!"

All that sinew and loud talk, the jockstraps launched across the aisle, the stupid stomping that preceded the *aaaaAAAAAWWW!* of their war cry.

And, under it all, the pleasant numbing rumble of large wheels on slippery asphalt, the pewter smell of exhaust mingled with the bus driver's smell of sweat and cigarettes—and, in every direction, farmland or forest or some other kind of nothing. The letters of my name, written in the condensed breath of boys on the bus windows, dissolved in little rivulets.

It was my freshman year. Miles Kruger, who was doing a dumb dance with a basketball jersey wrapped around his waist in imitation of a cheerleader's skirt, pumped his pelvis and sang in falsetto, "Extra extra, that's our team! Extra fast with lots of steam!"

When the bus driver hit the brakes for something black that had scurried onto the road, everyone on the bus fell forward, then backward, in a movement so fluid, it could have been choreographed. But the bus ran over it anyway, and there was a dull thump when it struck, and then the rising and falling of bus-weight over something large but soft. "Score!" Miles Kruger shouted, punching his fist at the air.

At this, we groaned in disapproval, shook our heads. "You're sick," one of the cheerleaders said. It might have been me. There was a supportive chorus of *yeah*s. And then the predictable chorus of boys mocking it: *"Yeah! You're sick, Miles."*

But we were girls, and we loved animals. We owned puppies and kittens. We tacked pictures of horses to our bedroom walls. It was inconceivable that anyone could joke about the death of an animal—proof that these boys were an alien race. An inferior one. Melody Hirsch actually set her lower lip to quivering. She was going to cry. Another girl reached over and took Melody's hand.

Melody Hirsch was, of all the cheerleaders, the greatest lover of animals. She wore a pin with a picture of a baby seal on it every day, and once a month collected money for the Save Our Seals fund.

"Fuck you, Miles," a cheerleader said, mostly for Melody's sake.

"Fuck you, Miles," the boys sang out in their falsettos.

Miles Kruger: Laid out on the shiny gym floor under the host team's score board, a few of its letters sizzling with some kind of electrical short, the score frozen at *Home: 27, Away: 8.* A heart condition he never knew he had.

Surprise!

Death.

Miles Kruger had the ball and was dribbling it down the court, but then he lost it and stumbled after it, and then, like a pilgrim having traveled on foot for many miles to a shrine, collapsed to his knees before it.

Someone blew a whistle, and we all froze in our places, and Coach Lewis jogged over to Miles and rolled him over, shouted something into his face and began to push on his chest.

Then, for a moment, gruesomely, it looked as though Coach Lewis were leaning into Miles Kruger for a tender kiss on the lips—but he was only breathing into his mouth.

When the paramedics finally arrived, they

attached a defibrillator to his chest, and briefly it seemed that Miles Kruger had been zapped back to life, arms flying off the floor, eyes wide open, a loud *buff* issuing from his lungs—a stunned boy, electrified, a body out there all alone trying desperately to come back to life. It looked as if some huge and invisible source of energy had yanked him off the floor, then tossed him back down. Done with him. Done forever with Miles Kruger.

He grew more still.

And heavier.

Miles Kruger became a thing *made* of weight. We could all see how incredibly heavy he had become by the expressions on the paramedics' faces as they wrenched him onto the stretcher from the floor.

They took him away, and the host team's cheerleaders hurried us into the girls' locker room. They left quickly, leaving our squad alone together, sitting on aluminum locker room benches, surrounded by our hosts' padlocks, the smell of their foreign perspiration, their shampoo and soap, in silence for more than an hour while official business took place in the hallway.

Parents were phoned. Papers were signed.

The wild hiccuping sound of boys' sobbing. Time passed slowly, like a pearl sinking to the depths of a bottle of thick green shampoo. Someone outside the girls' locker room was saying a prayer. It sounded like *hullabaloo hullabaloo hullabaloo* being repeated over and over. But inside the girls' locker room there was just silence in the muggy cold as our upper arms and thighs grew mottled with chill and stillness.

Now and then, a whisper, a cleared throat, a quivering sigh.

And then, a giggle.

A stifled laugh.

And then a joke muttered just under one girl's breath—so brutal and outrageous, all the rules of the Athletic Code of Conduct, of girlhood and school spirit and sweetness and feminine restraint so blithely violated—that we all grew wild with it.

Hands to our mouths, trying not to laugh so loud, so hard, but crumpled with it anyway, gasping, as the laughter grew louder, freer, more dangerous as it went on and on and on.

Any one of us might have said it, but Melody Hirsch was the one who did:

"Score," she said.

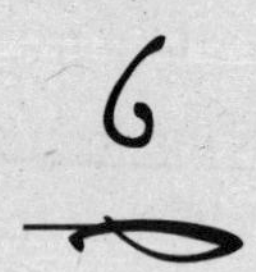

I could see the driver most clearly. He was dark-haired, wearing a plaid shirt with short sleeves. His hair was long and straggly. Leaning around to see over his shoulder was another boy wearing an orange cap.

"Don't give them the satisfaction," Desiree said. "They've been sitting there staring at us since they pulled in."

"Grubs," the other Kristi said from the backseat. It was a word she'd already used several times in the last two days—a word we didn't use in East Grand Rapids, but which she said meant "grubby" or "gross." There was, she said, a whole clique of Grubs at Crystal River High, and they wore chains in their belts, marijuana leaf belt buckles, got shitty grades, and sat together in the cafeteria.

"Metalheads," Desiree said.

I could hear their radio playing. The sappy wailing of electric guitars, and some guy singing in falsetto.

No, they weren't really metalheads, I thought. They were just hicks. Their idling station wagon was loud. It probably belonged to one of their mothers, and the smell that drifted over from it was deeply acrid. Stagnant. But also smokily sweet—redolent of machine and mystery and molten rock and metal at the core of the earth. A grayish tail of exhaust poured from the muffler.

I realized, then, that it was true what they said—that it was possible to *feel* boys' eyes on you. I'd known they were there even before Desiree had pointed them out. I'd *felt* them looking—those warm zeros passing over my legs and breasts as I'd leaned against my Mustang licking salt and caramel off my fingers. That had been them, that slightly warm but also weak sensation of a doctor's penlight moving around my body, searching for something.

"Jesus!" Desiree said, shaking her head in exasperation. "Don't *smile* at them."

Had I smiled?

Yes, I realized, I had—because the smile was still on my face, and I was still looking in their direction, and the driver, the one in the plaid shirt, had leaned over his steering wheel with wide eyes, as if he could scarcely believe it, and he was smiling back.

"Christ," the redhead said. "Don't even *acknowledge* them."

"*Really*," Desiree said. "Why did you *smile*?" She let her jaw hang open for effect, and I could see the inside of her mouth. It was a slippery red cave with a string of pearls in it.

"Let's just get out of here," the redhead said, "before they come over here and try to talk to us."

"Yeah," said Desiree, "except that now they'll probably follow us around for the rest our lives, thanks to Smiley Face here."

"Okay, okay," I said, holding my hands up off the steering wheel. "I'm sorry. Shoot me, okay, I'm nice."

Desiree made a pistol out of her hand, pointed it between my eyes, and said, "Bang."

But it was true.

I *was* nice.

Everyone said so.

Friendly. Outgoing. I'd been taught to smile—for the camera, for the old people, for the crowd. I'd been smiling spontaneously since I was six years old, a flower girl at my mother's wedding to my stepfather. They told me that the most important thing to do was smile, that the things I was worried about (stumbling, walking down the aisle out of time to the music) wouldn't matter at all as long as I remembered to smile.

So I smiled. There were photographs to prove it: Me in a butter-yellow silk dress with ribbons in my hair. A wicker basket full of flower petals. Walking down an aisle. Big smile.

The petals had been waxy and cool to the touch, as if they were sweating. I was scared, and my mother had to give me a little push to get me going when the organist started the wedding march. But once I was out there, smiling, I was all flower girl, aware of nothing but the permanent importance of that smile and the sound of my dress rustling. The scared girl I'd been, she was gone. *She* was hovering around near the ceiling lights, held up by the warm breath of the people watching me from their pews, looking down at this other girl, this smiling *me,* as if the whole scene were already a photograph pressed into an album. A memory. "*Smile,*" my mother had said, pushing me into the aisle.

And how many times during every cheerleading practice had we been told—screamed at, commanded, *threatened*—to smile?

"That's all you've got," Margo would tell us. "You've got a routine you might forget, a team that might lose, ankles that might sprain, uniforms that might get dirty. It might be pouring rain or snowing out there, and the only thing you can guarantee me you can do in spite of it all is *smile.*

"And, frankly girls, that's all a cheerleader *absolutely has to do.*"

But some girls couldn't. They might be able to fake it for tryouts one year and get on the squad, but they wouldn't be chosen for the next season no matter what their back-flips were like. They could cartwheel one-handed from one end of the field to the other, but if they weren't smiling at the end of it, Margo would be standing there when they got done to narrow her eyes and shake her head.

I was not one of those girls.

I knew how to smile. And I'd smiled at the

boys in the rusty station wagon because that's what I did. Naturally. Involuntarily. Without even knowing I was doing it.

Now, I could see in the rearview mirror that they were only a few feet behind us, and both of them were smiling now too. Smiling back. At me. The one in the passenger seat had taken off his orange cap and was smoothing down his messy blond hair. The driver was drumming his fingers excitedly on the steering wheel. Behind me, the redhead swiveled around quickly and said, "Shit. We've got company."

"Just drive, Smiley Face," Desiree said. "The damage is done, but they're not going to keep up with us, driving that bucket of rust, *if* you *step* on it."

"Okay," I said, "okay," and pulled my knees closer together to keep the bottle between them from spilling, and then I stepped on the gas pedal hard, peeling out of the Standard Station parking lot so fast that the back tires of my red Mustang squealed and burned over the blacktop, leaving two oily sashes behind them on the warm tar, like two black scarves—or like shadows slapped onto shadow.

Two

"Where did you go?"

I turned around fast. It was Slippery Lips. She'd appeared out of nowhere, or so it seemed to me. I was standing with my back to the door in the quiet and pinkly chemical dankness of the girls' room, waiting for Desiree to finish washing her face, and intently watching a spider spin an elaborate web between the window frame and the screen of a shoebox-sized window over the sink.

It seemed pathetic to me, and incredibly shortsighted of that spider, to build something so intricate there. All it would take was one cheerleader who thought the bathroom was too cold slamming the window shut to wreck everything.

Still, for now, something brown wriggled at the center of it—which was, I supposed, the point of a spider's web.

It wasn't a home. It wasn't permanent. It was a trap.

When Slippery Lips spoke, I turned around to find her right behind me, her ash-brown hair pulled up in a severe bun, wearing her wire-rimmed glasses and looking a little like an angry ballerina.

"We had to go to town," Desiree answered for me from the sink, her voice muffled by water and porcelain. She was dragging a white washcloth across her forehead. "That other Kristi," Desiree said, "the one with the red hair, she got her period and didn't have any—"

"Tampons?" Slippery Lips finished Desiree's sentence for her as a question, then put her hands on her hips. "You've got to be kidding me," she said. Her aquamarine eyes narrowed behind her glasses. They reminded me of the eyes of a Siamese cat that had briefly lived next door to us. That cat had been unbelievably beautiful—a long, arched back, pearl-gray fur, tail always poised over itself in a question mark. But when I'd tried to pet it once, it scratched me right down my arm from the underside of my elbow to my palm as if it had wanted to kill me—as if it knew *how*. I still had the scar, now just a thin seam that showed up because the skin on the underside of my arm was so pale.

"This is a cheerleading camp," Slippery Lips said. "You think we don't have about five thousand boxes of tampons here?"

Desire straightened up from the sink. She shrugged, and then turned from the mirror to Slippery Lips and shook out her golden hair. There were surprisingly bright strands mixed in with the damper, darker hair. They looked like something spun miraculously *out* of hair, too luminous to simply be hair.

"We told her that," Desiree said, "but she claimed she had to have some special *kind* of tampon, that the applicators of the tampons in the dispensers were too dry or something. She was afraid to use Vaseline to slide them in."

"Oh," the counselor said. Satisfied. The Vaseline. "Okay."

I exhaled.

It was amazing.

Desiree was *so brilliant* when it came to lying, so adept at snatching the perfect detail out of thin air every time. How did she do it? I knew that if it had been left to me, I'd have found myself telling the truth no matter how hard I'd tried not to—*We didn't want to do sit-ups, so we we were going to go skinny-dipping in Lovers' Lake, but then . . .*

"Did you get them?"

"No," Desiree answered, shaking her head with what looked like genuine regret. "They didn't have them at the gas station, and we were worried we were going to get in trouble for being gone, so we didn't drive all the way into town."

"Oh," the counselor said. "Where is she?"

"She's lying down back in the cabin," I said. It was true.

"Okay, okay," Slippery Lips said. "You two get ready for Free Swim. Put on your bathing suits and meet the others outside the dining hall. And don't *ever* leave this camp again without telling one of us where you're going and getting a *signed* permission slip, okay?"

"Sure," Desiree said, as if it were self-evident.

When Slippery Lips turned her back to walk out of the girls' room, Desiree raised her middle finger to the counselor's back.

2

In elementary school, Desiree taught me how to dab just a tiny bit of soap into the corners of my eyes, into the little bloody triangles near the bridge of my nose, to make it look like I was crying.

It helped, she explained, when you were in trouble. At home. At school. Wherever. Tears always made whatever excuse you were trying to present more believable. But because it was hard to cry on demand, sometimes you needed a bit of soap in your eyes, and Desiree knew how to apply it so that it only hurt a little but turned your eyes pink and urged a few hot tears to burn out of them.

It was a trick I only used once, mainly because

my mother, unlike Desiree's, didn't have that kind of soft-spot for tears. But the one occasion I'd needed it, Desiree was right: it worked like a charm. I was in fifth grade. After recess, I hurried into the girls' room, dabbed a bit of the pink soap onto the tips of my index fingers, pressed it into the corners of my eyes, and stumbled out of the girls' room into the gray hallway of Lakeside Elementary school, streaming with tears.

"What happened?" my teacher Mrs. Matthews cried out, rushing over.

My white dress was splattered from the collar to the hem with mud.

"He pushed me," I said, pointing my finger at David Strang, who'd just walked through the orange double doors on his way in from the playground.

David Strang looked over at me and then at Mrs. Matthews, with terror on his face—mouth wide open, hands raised in front of him as if he were trying to show everyone that they were empty. "I—" was all he had a chance to say before Mrs. Matthews marched straight over to him, grabbed him by the arm, and said, "You're in big trouble, young man."

I'd had to do it.

He *had* chased me—although he hadn't *pushed* me. Instead, while he was chasing me, I'd tripped on a tree root, and the white dress my great aunt Eileen had sewn for me in the months before she'd died, the dress my mother had told me not to wear to school, was suddenly splattered with mud. I'd had to beg and plead to wear it, and as I'd left the house that morning, my mother warned me that if I ruined that white dress, I was going to be one very sorry little girl.

I hadn't felt bad about the lie until I saw, as David Strang was being marched into the principal's office by Mrs. Matthews, the way the tail of his white shirt, sweaty and wrinkled, had worked its way out of his pants, and how his buzzed-short blond hair under the fluorescent lights of the hallway seemed to reveal a pale and fragile skull.

He denied and cried, but in the end his mother agreed to pay for my dress to be dry-cleaned—and although my own mother had sighed and put her hands on her hips and shook her head, she didn't punish me. Mrs. Matthews assured her that it hadn't been my fault:

He pushed me.

After a while, it seemed to me he really had.

I could even feel it, his hand on my back—although he hadn't even been close.

And the tree root, swelling its knobbiness out of the dirt, a mangled half-buried limb—I could still see that tree root and the shiny toe of my black shoe catching itself against the gray bark, but after a while it seemed to me that these two incidents were separate.

I was pushed, and the more David Strang denied it, the more I came to believe it was true.

Those soapy tears became as real to me, in my memory, as any tears I'd ever cried.

Everyone else believed them, too, because no one ever believed a boy.

The sun grew hotter in the sky as the afternoon progressed, and where we walked along the path to Free Swim, it filtered through a muggy lime-green canopy of needles and leaves. Little gnats hovered in the air around our heads like busy halos—living ashes, animated punctuation marks—and the ringing of the cicadas became a kind of glassy barrier, a windshield between the earth and heaven.

I was tired. Hungry. Light-headed.

We'd sneaked out before lunch, and all I'd had to eat since breakfast was that Pay Day. It was a longer walk to the lake than I remembered from the year before.

The heat, dizzying.

Captured under that rigid ceiling of cicada whine was the smell of flesh coated in insect repellent mixed with tanning oil. This combined with the smell of the forest, a mulchy decay that arose from the ground and was passed over by twenty-seven pairs of flip-flops.

At first I couldn't decide what the sound of all those flip-flops together reminded me of.

Gulping? Soft wings flapping? The sound of an enormous dog lapping water from a puddle?

But then I realized that it was the sound of kissing.

Wild, sloppy kissing taking place in a crowd.

Hypnotic. That kissing sound.

The walking. The flip-flops. The smell of pine and flesh. The cicada drone overhead. No one was talking. We were simply a herd of girls being marched down to a watery hole at the center of the Blanc Coeur National Forest.

"*Blanc Coeur,*" Slippery Lips had explained on the first night for the benefit of those new to Pine Ridge Cheerleading Camp, "means 'White Heart' in French." She'd gone on to tell us that it had been named by a French explorer who, two hundred years before, had set out with three other men and an Indian guide. They had walked through the forest into what would eventually become the dumpy little town of St. Sophia (a place which, as far as I could tell, had nothing in it except some bars, a couple of churches, a casket company, and some gas stations). The other guys and the Indian died during the trek.

"So, why did he name it the 'White Heart'?" I asked.

Slippery Lips raised and lowered her shoulders as though it had never crossed her mind to wonder.

Desiree looked back at me and shook her head. "Come on, Slowpoke," she said, but I was too tired to hurry. The bugs around my face. The cicada whine. The powdery dirt beneath my flip-flops was booby-trapped with tree roots. I saw a log a few feet off the path, surrounded by ferns, coated with a veil of shimmering emerald, looking as if some magical forest creature had passed over it with a basket of jewels, and sprinkled it all over with a wand. I thought about going to it, sitting down, but remembered Slippery Lips saying, "When you are in the forest, do *not* go off the path *no matter what.*" She'd told us a little story to scare us, a story about a cheerleader who *had* wandered off the path and has *never been found.* And that cheerleader, Slippery Lips told us, had wandered off the path *in 1967.*

We had been sitting up in our cots when she told us the story. The lights were out, but every girl had a flashlight burning in her lap. We were all very quiet when she was done. We knew that if that girl had been out there in the Blanc Coeur National Forest for so many years, she wasn't coming back—and also that, in one form or another, that girl was still out there, which was another excellent reason never to wander off the path.

Some rules needed to be emphasized, and some were so self-evident, it amazed me that anyone ever broke them, that anyone had ever needed to make a rule in the first place:

Don't drink lake water. Don't play with matches. Don't talk with your mouth full. Don't eat food you find on the ground. Don't take candy from strangers.

"People are so stupid," my mother sometimes said. She'd be waiting for the driver in front of us to notice that the light had turned green. Or sometimes she'd say instead, "People can be so crazy," referring to murders, wars, or sightings of UFOs, or to my grandmother, her mother, who'd spent half her life in a mental institution because no one could convince her that there were no "shadow people" trying to lure her out of the house in the middle of the night.

"I'd wake up," my mother told me, "when I was fourteen, fifteen, and she'd be standing at the front door trying to reason with the 'shadow people.' 'No,' she'd be whispering, 'I can't come out. You come in here.' The cops would bring her home when they found her standing in the middle of Wildwood Avenue arguing with no one."

It was hard to imagine, on the few occasions I saw my grandmother at Springbrook Rest Home, that she'd ever been capable of arguing with anyone, let alone *no one*. By then she was just a blank-eyed mannequin in a wheelchair. When she said anything at all, it was, "Oh, dear." And then she died when I was nine.

But the "shadow people" had lodged in my imagination. I pictured them as silhouettes. Silhouettes that wanted to play. Silhouettes that had tempted my grandmother out of her house every night because they were bored, and because she could see them, when no one else could.

"If there are ghosts," my mother used to say when I was very little and worried about them, "why hasn't any sane person ever seen one?"

I'd fallen behind. Desiree and the others had rounded a corner and were out of sight ahead of me. Some were still on the path. I could hear their flip-flops. But some had already gotten down to the lake. I could hear splashing, laughing, and a whistle, a male voice shouting—the lifeguard down at the Free Swim lake. Some cheerleader must have tried to swim past the buoys. I started to run, to catch up with the others. I did not want to be out there alone—to turn and see that cheerleader standing in the shadows, still wearing her love beads and bell-bottoms. Or the ghost of that French explorer. Or a bear. Or any other surprise. When I reached the end of the path and saw the bright bikinis and shining hair of the other cheerleaders, I was out of breath but happy to be back among them.

"What happened to you?" Desiree asked when I got down to the sandy little beach. She was lying with her legs spread out on a Barbie beach towel—a souvenir from her childhood, which had been entirely devoted to Barbies.

"I had to slow down," I said. "I'm exhausted. Aren't you?"

"I was," Desiree said, "until I saw *him*."

She nodded in the direction of the lake, which was a blue-black hole with a white rope and red buoys bobbing at the center. On a white dock, a boy with blond hair and a strip of zinc oxide across his nose was standing, twirling a whistle on a rope. He was wearing a bathing suit decorated with stars and stripes.

"Lifeguard," Desiree said in a low voice meant to sound foreign and sultry but sounding, instead, hoarse.

She motioned toward him with her tongue. "Angel Boy," she said.

Angel Boy was Desiree's nickname for any attractive boy who was blond. Darker boys, attractive ones, were *Devil Boys*.

The ringing of the cicadas and the harsh light of sun on the lake made this Angel Boy look as if he were standing on the opposite side of a shining abyss. It was hard to look directly at him without squinting, so it became impossible to see him in any detail, as if a curtain of summer had been drawn down between this lifeguard and the beach. Desiree said, "I think I'm going for a little dip. It's *awfully* hot," and stood up, then looked down at me. "How about you?"

I tossed my towel on the sand, kicked my flip-flops off, and followed her down to the water.

The sand was burning, and the sun had caused a mirage of wrinkled cellophane to rise from the place where the lake met the shore. I stepped closer to the water and looked down at a wet tangle of seaweed that was being washed up and pulled back out, and when I looked up again, Desiree was gone, having slipped straight into the lake headfirst.

The suddenness of it, the stillness of the lake both before and after she disappeared in it, made it seem as if she'd simply come to the edge of the water and slipped straight out of her skin.

But in only a few seconds, Desiree had sputtered up again near the dock where Angel Boy was twirling his silver whistle, which glinted painfully in the sun. He'd seen her, it seemed, and had been scanning the lake for her after she dove in. When she emerged, shaking her hair and rubbing the water out of her eyes, he reached down and took her hand to help her up onto the dock.

From where I stood, up to my ankles in the water, I watched them, using my hand as a visor to block the sun. Their shadows tangled off the edge of the dock and wavered on the water between two bobbing buoys, which were held up by a white rope distinguishing the part of the lake that was safe for swimming from the part that wasn't. Desiree's blond hair streamed with water down her back, and she had one hand on her hip. Her back was to me, and I could see the diamonds of water on her skin, the way they lit up each cool bump of her spine.

Together, Desiree and the lifeguard looked like a strange flag—he in his stars-and-stripes suit, and she in her navy blue bikini—a flag held together with flesh.

My father, my *first* father, went away and never came back. He wasn't exactly missing in action because they'd seen the plane he had been flying crash into the side of a mountain and they had found his dog tags in some ashes where it had crashed. But there was nothing to bury, so there'd been a memorial service with an empty casket and, draped over it, a flag.

I remembered wondering what was in the casket because I'd never seen one before and I didn't know they usually had bodies in them. I remembered seeing a man in a uniform like my father's try to hand the folded-up flag to my mother, who wouldn't take it. He handed it to my grandmother instead, and she kept it in a trunk in the attic and took it out only three times a year—on Memorial Day, Veterans' Day, and the Fourth of July—to fly it. She told me that when she died she wanted me to have the flag, to have something to remember my father by, but I had no idea where it had gone when she really did die and, with or without the flag, had almost no memory at all of my first father—only one fragmented glimpse of him with his head tilted at the dining room table, his ear cocked in the direction of the roof. He was a pilot, we were living on an air force base, and he must have been listening for a plane, but in my memory he was being spoken to by someone from the sky.

"It was noisy," my mother told me when I described that memory to her. "Day and night. Landing and taking off. Maybe he was trying to hear something one of us was saying, and he couldn't." She was being sarcastic.

But it was the only real image I had of him, except one I'd gotten from a photograph my grandmother kept in her bedroom of my father in uniform, his foot resting on the bumper of a car with brake lights that looked like cat's eyes. Sometimes, when I visited her in Indiana (one week, every summer), I would go into the bedroom while she was making dinner and look at that photograph. Just stare at it and wonder:

Had I ever actually *seen* him?

Was the man in that photograph really, in any way, related to me?

His shoe on the bumper was shiny, and he looked handsome and young, and his eyes in the fading Kodak blue were exactly the color of my own.

My grandmother had never gotten over it, my cousins told me. Not even a few ashes to scatter in the backyard. Every inch of wall space that was not taken up with depictions of suffering Jesuses or swooning Madonnas had some image of my father on it.

As a boy with a baseball.

A grainy black-and-white baby shaking a blurred rattle at the camera.

A teenager in a white dinner jacket and black pants getting ready to go to some dance.

Although I had only that one memory of him, I had a few vague memories of the years before he was gone for good, memories of the air force base where I'd been born and where we'd lived until I was five years old. One of them was a memory of a Fourth of July after he had been gone for a long time but wasn't yet dead, when I'd decorated my bike with red, white, and blue crepe paper and little American flags and ridden it around the base with the other air force brats in an impromptu parade.

If I concentrated, I could still hear the sound of that crepe paper rustling dryly behind my bike, the snap and hush of those fragile strips trailing me.

Everything else about the air force base was something I'd been told by my mother, who'd hated it. The noise. The neighbors who argued for hours every night. The old Cajun woman who watched me in the afternoons when my mother went to work and who told her that she'd had a premonition that my father was never going to come back.

"You mean he'll be back in a body bag? He'll be killed?" my mother told me she'd asked the old woman, and that the old woman had said, "No. He'll just never come back."

"I fired her after that," my mother said. "She

was right, in the end, I guess, but I didn't want to have her watching my child."

I was too little to remember that old woman, but sometimes I pictured my bedroom in the house on that base and an old lady in the corner of it rocking in a chair as I woke slowly from a nap. I pictured her with a flag draped over her lap, a needle and thread in her hands, as if she'd been mending it, or making it, as I slept.

5

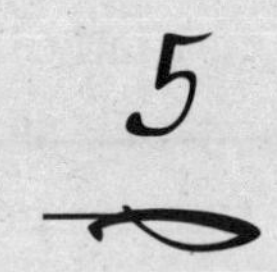

The walk back from Free Swim was even hotter and stickier than the walk to it had been. The cicadas were buzzing more loudly, seeming lower in the trees, and the lake water had coated my skin with something salty and rank to which the flies and gnats were hopelessly attracted. They circled my body hungrily, landing on my back and calves, hovering around my hair and eyes. I put my hand over my mouth, afraid to breathe in the tiny flying ashes of them. When the blackflies bit, it was as if small electrical shocks were flashing on my bare skin.

And I wasn't the only one. We'd all left our cans of Off! back in the cabins and were slapping, whining, screeching, "Ouch!" and "Shit!" We'd wrapped ourselves in beach towels to expose as little flesh as possible to the flies, and hurried as fast as we could in our flip-flops on the dirt path, like a platoon of cheerleaders being pursued by an army of flies.

All of us were being pursued, it seemed, except for Desiree, who had her towel tied in a knot around her waist and was walking casually behind the rest of us, being bitten and chased by nothing.

When I looked back at her, she gave me a sleepy smile.

She'd spent all of the Free Swim period on the dock with the lifeguard, pretending to sunbathe, but it was obvious that she was only there to lay her body at his feet. For a while she'd been spread out on her back with her hair fanned around her and one leg bent. Then she rolled over and untied the straps of her bikini top and lay for a long time with her naked back glistening up at him.

Still, the lifeguard had somehow managed to keep doing his job—blowing his whistle when a cheerleader swam under the rope or answering some question that Slippery Lips shouted to him from the beach about where the drop-off began.

But when he wasn't scanning the surface of the water for trouble, he seemed to be working hard not to stare at Desiree.

After a while, I got bored, and decided to go out there, too. It had gotten hot and I wanted to swim, but the bottom of the lake was so soft under my feet when I waded into it that I felt as if I were walking across a murky cloud. It rose up around my calves in velvety explosions when I nudged it with my toes. I managed to walk into the water up to my breasts, but I turned back when I felt something cool and fast slide between my thighs. I looked back to see a fish, nearly a foot long and pure black, cutting its way through the water without a sound—a thick arrow made of flesh. I couldn't help but think of the redhead's leeches, so I ended up spending the rest of Free Swim on my beach towel, digging my toes into the gritty sand, waiting for Desiree—who, I knew, would not leave the dock until Free Swim was officially over.

I sat and watched them. The lifeguard's back was a ripple of muscle in the sunlight, and Desiree looked like a living shadow at his feet. I wished she would sit up and look for me, but I knew she wouldn't. And that lifeguard—I'd have to be drowning before he would notice me either.

I wasn't jealous, exactly. Not of the lifeguard. Or even of Desiree's perfect body at his feet. If I was jealous at all, it was of the way she knew what she wanted and went after it while I was always stuck just trying to figure out what I wanted.

Like Tony Sparrow.

He'd passed me a note in seventh grade that asked, "Do you want to go with me?" I put the note in my pocket.

Did I want to "go" with Tony Sparrow?

I had no idea.

I knew that "going" with a boy meant standing around with him a lot in the hallway, maybe walking home from school together or sitting beside him during a school assembly. And it seemed like the kind of thing a girl would want to do with Tony Sparrow. He was the most popular boy in the school. The best looking. Funny, in a mean way. And rich. That week, I took the note out a few times and looked at it again, trying to decide what I wanted to do about it. And then, that Saturday night when Desiree called up while I was watching television with my mother and told me she'd just had sex with Tony Sparrow, I realized that whatever decision I was going to make, it was too late to make it.

And, even now, although I'd been going with Chip Chase off and on for two years, we'd done nothing more than kiss and rub our bodies against each other on the couch in my basement. A few times, he'd put his hand up my shirt. I wasn't sure if I wanted anything else, and he didn't seem to know, either.

"Slowpoke." Desiree elbowed me gently in the ribs as she passed me on the path. Her back was bare and dry.

I watched it, that familiar plane, as she cut ahead of the other girls and disappeared. It seemed to me that the ringing of the cicadas didn't even follow her as it did the rest of us.

"She doesn't waste any time, does she?" a girl behind me asked.

I turned.

She was a stocky, muscular girl I hadn't noticed before, and her long dark shadow stretched behind her in a deformed silhouette.

"Your friend," she nodded ahead of us on the

path. "She's pretty fast, isn't she?"

"She's a slut. So what?" I said, turning my back to her.

"Right," the stocky girl said under her breath behind me. "So what."

When I got back to my cabin I was startled to see the other Kristi lying in her cot. I'd forgotten about her, and the cramps, and that she'd been excused from Free Swim. She was deep inside her sleeping bag with the drawstring pulled up to her chin, but wide awake. She said nothing when I came in. There were frantic shadows chasing each other around on the ceiling—leaves, sunlight—and she seemed to be watching those.

"Are you okay?" I asked.

I tossed my towel on the floor at the foot of my cot and pulled down the bottoms of my bikini. They clung around my knees in a damp tangle and I had to sit down on my cot to get them all the way off.

"No," she said.

"Did you get some tampons?"

"Yeah," she said.

"Are you going to dinner?"

"No," she said.

There was a fat fly circling a wad of toilet paper on the floor next to her cot, and I wondered if she'd wrapped a used tampon in there and not bothered to put it in the trash, if the fly was circling the smell of her blood.

I stood up and stepped into my panties, put my bikini on the windowsill, pulled my shorts up, my T-shirt on, and said, "Okay. I hope you . . ." but I could think of nothing else to say. I turned around. The other girls were just coming into the cabin, the screen door slamming behind them. I was about to start making my way to the door when she said, "I saw those grubs. They followed us here."

"What?" I asked.

She sat up and beckoned me toward her, and when I leaned over she grabbed my upper arm so tightly it stung. "They were standing outside the cabin," she said, pointing to the window screen above my cot. "Right there. And they were watching me, and when I screamed they took off into the woods."

Her breath smelled like cinnamon, sweet and hot at the same time. I stepped away from her and pulled my arm out of her grip, and when I did I could see the outline of her fingerprints burned white into my flesh. I backed up, shaking my head. I said, "No way," and laughed a little through my nose.

"Right there," she said, pointing again, and I could see that her hand was shaking. The other cheerleaders were taking off their bikinis, giggling at something one of them had said, paying no attention to us.

"Look," I said, still looking at her but bending over to tie one of my shoes. The laces were so new they wouldn't stay knotted. "I don't want to make you feel bad," I said, "but that's nuts. You didn't see those guys. Even if they tried to follow us, they could never have caught up, and they had no way of knowing where we were going, anyway. Maybe you just need something to eat, or— "

"I'll go to dinner with you," she said, sitting up.

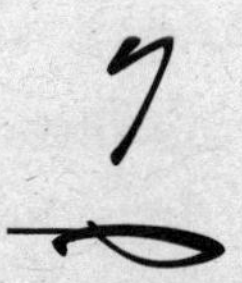

The dining hall was already full of girls waiting in line with their empty plates by the time we got there. It had taken the other Kristi a long time to change into fresh clothes, and afterward she'd had to go to the bathroom, where she washed her hands and raked the pink comb through her hair twenty or thirty times.

"You can go without me," she'd said when I crossed my arms impatiently and leaned against the cinder block, but I said I was in no hurry.

I could see, above the sinks, that I'd been right.

Someone had shut the window, and the spider's web was just a few crushed strands with a dead bug tangled in it now.

When we finally got to dinner, the meal was

laid out on a long Formica-topped table, and appeared to be potato salad along with thin gray slices of meat curled at the edges. I couldn't help wondering what it was.

Pig? Cow? Horse?

The gray meat in the silver tureen could have been anything, and at first I hesitated to put it on my plate. But I was hungry enough to eat it, whatever it was.

"I'm not eating that," Kristi said. There was nothing but a spoonful of potato salad on her plate.

"I *have* to eat it," I said. "I'm starving."

"I'd rather starve," she said. "Where should we sit?"

I nodded toward the table where I'd glimpsed Desiree's blond hair shining in a shaft of sunlight that was pouring through the dining hall screens. The lifeguard was beside her. When the redhead saw who I was nodding toward, she sighed as if at the sight of something too exhausting for words, but she headed in Desiree's direction with her tray anyway. I followed her long red ponytail over to the table. She was wearing a sleeveless shirt, and, walking behind her, I could see that even her shoulders were freckled, the pure white skin looking as if it had been spattered with blood.

"Hi," Desiree said, looking up at us. She was moving a forkful of potato salad around on her plate in dreamy circles. She'd changed into a tight white T-shirt that said "Bahama Mama" on it in orange cursive. I had one just like it back home. We'd bought them together the year before when we'd gone to the Bahamas with the Pep Club for spring break.

It had only been a three-night, four-day trip, paid for by months of Pep Club fund-raising (bake sales, car washes, concession stand popcorn), but it passed so quickly, in such a blur of blue water and pina coladas, that I remembered almost nothing of it—just that the hotel we'd stayed in had been enormous and pink, and the sandy beach beyond it blindingly white, and that whoever our parental chaperones were, they disappeared soon after we checked in. Desiree and I spent our four afternoons together tanning on the beach, and our first two nights at a discotheque called Dreamland, dancing and drinking.

"You're old enough to buy a drink in the Bahamas if you can reach the bar," my stepfather had told me. "We expect you to use good judgment."

In truth, you didn't need to be able to reach the bar because you could order a drink from your lounge chair or your towel on the beach without ever standing up at all. And, having never had so much alcohol available to me before (just a snitched bottle of wine, a few Budweisers bought with a fake ID at a convenience store now and then, some cups of guzzled beer from a keg before someone's parents got home and busted us), using judgment, good or bad, seemed secondary to drinking as much as possible while it was still available.

Desiree had brought a Polaroid camera with her. After the second night at Dreamland, I woke up thirsty and dizzy with my head throbbing from a dream in which I'd been asked, as part of a cheerleading routine, to jump through a hoop of fire. Desiree brought me aspirin and showed me a Polaroid of myself kissing a tall black man in a salmon pink suit.

It was definitely Dreamland.

I recognized that much—the pastel Christmas lights strung along the sweaty cement walls.

I also recognized the bartender in the background waving into the camera's flash, his dark skin shimmering with sweat. (His name had been Albert, and he was missing two teeth in his brilliant smile. "Got knocked out with a bottle," he'd told us the first night, holding a bottle in his fist to demonstrate, swinging it in the direction of his own smile.)

And I recognized myself in this Polaroid from Dreamland. The red halter-top dress with the fringed hem, my hair pinned up at the back of my neck, a few curls cascading out of it. That was my back, my arm, the side of my face pressed into the tall handsome black man's face.

But who was *he,* and when had we kissed?

"That's Gregory," Desiree said, pointing to him in the photo. "You promised to marry him. Remember?"

The man's suit was the slick pink of the underside of a conch shell. He had one hand at the back of my neck and one hand on my hip.

"Jesus," I said. "How many pina coladas did I drink?"

"Many," Desiree said. "*Many*. You wanted to go home with him and meet his mother— "

"Oh my God."

"—but luckily you passed out in the bathroom and Josh French carried you back here." I gasped. "Don't worry," she reassured me. "I didn't leave you alone with Josh."

Josh French was the son of the football coach. He owned a van out of which he sold drugs, and in which he was rumored to have orgies with girls from the junior high. It was said that Josh French had caused an epidemic of syphilis to sweep through East Grand Rapids. I'd always assumed that the rumor was true and had made a mental note at parties not to sit on any toilet seat that Josh French or any of his girlfriends might have sat on.

I looked more closely at myself in the photograph.

The last thing I remembered about the evening was stumbling while dancing in my high heels, bumping into a railing or a table. That's where my memory of the evening ended.

But there I was in that Polaroid—myself, but also a stranger. The night had gone on, it seemed, for many hours, both with me and without me.

I'd been there, but *who* had I been?

I vowed to myself right then never to drink

that much again, and I never did. Our last night in the Bahamas, Desiree and I went to a different disco because she said that the man in the pink suit had promised to meet me at Dreamland as soon as the sun set, to continue making the plans we'd begun the night before.

At the the other disco, Cosmos, I didn't drink or dance at all, and I couldn't help but think about that man waiting for me back in Dreamland, thinking he knew who I was. I felt, somehow, the presence of myself there with him, dancing and kissing, making plans—a kind of ghost, or shadow, as if some part of myself had slipped away from me and was living its own life somewhere else.

And it scared me.

Maybe it was the hangover, the bad sunburn that had caused my shoulders to blister and made me feel as if I had a low-grade fever, but I couldn't shake the feeling that there, at Dreamland with Gregory, was another me, a *me* I couldn't control, a *me* who didn't even know I existed.

Now, Desiree pulled at the neck of her "Bahama Mama" T-shirt as if it were too tight. "This is T.J.," she said, nodding to the lifeguard at her side. "T.J., this is Kristy and also *Kristi*." She made sweeping gestures from one side of the table to the other to introduce us.

"Hi," he said to both of us at once. "Nice name."

"Thank you," we each said at the same time.

Without the strip of zinc oxide, I could see how perfectly chiseled his features were—except for a bump in the middle of his nose that made it look as if, once, the nose had been broken and had healed badly. But it was that bump that made him beautiful by keeping him from being too pretty—that and the fact that he had only one dimple. When he smiled, it made a small indentation on the left side of his face, causing him to look slightly lopsided. Sitting down across from him, I instinctively tilted my head to the right to see him straighter.

It was hard not to stare.

He might have been the most attractive boy I'd ever seen in my life.

His hair was just past his ears, the bangs looking as if he'd tried to comb them before dinner, but they were too blond and weightless to stay in place and had risen over his forehead in a cool bright fringe. He was wearing a white baseball jersey with a red band around the collar and solid red sleeves that came down to his elbows. The shirt said "Falcons" in loopy letters on his chest. Around his neck he wore a shark tooth on a leather shoelace. His dinner plate was empty. Whatever he'd taken, he'd already eaten. "Excuse me," he said, pushing his chair away from the table. "I have to—"

I looked away, embarrassed suddenly, wondering if he was leaving because I'd stared too long.

"I'm done too," Desiree said, and she rose with her dinner tray and followed T.J. away without bothering to say good-bye.

The other Kristi didn't say good-bye either. She was looking at her potato salad. She hadn't even seemed to notice that T.J. and Desiree were there, let alone that they'd left. She inhaled deeply through her nose, then looked up at me. "I can't eat this," she said.

This time, it did not sound so much like whining as a kind of desperation. She couldn't eat it. It was just a fact. And she must have been hungry—at least as hungry as I was, and I was ravenous. I was hungry enough to have eaten anything. She couldn't have had much more than a bowl of cornflakes that morning. The diet sodas we'd had from the gas station around noon had no calories, and as far as I knew she'd had nothing else to eat all day. All there was after dinner each night were a few marshmallows roasted at the ends of twigs around a campfire, and if she couldn't stomach the potato salad, I couldn't imagine she'd be able to eat those. I still didn't like her, but I felt sorry for her.

The meat was really *not* so bad—salty, but not too tough—although the potato salad was truly terrible. Since I'd dished it onto my plate it had begun to turn pink, as if it were trying to become something it wasn't. Jewelry. Flowers. Toes.

"It's not that bad," I said, trying to sound nice. "The meat's okay. Maybe they have some peanut butter? I saw a loaf of bread."

"Yeah," she said, and seemed to brighten a little, swallowing as if she'd decided at this suggestion that she would try not to cry after all.

It was strange, I thought, looking at her face, how you wouldn't think a girl covered in small red flecks could be so beautiful. It was not a detail you'd use to describe a truly beautiful person—but she was one. Freckled or not, she looked like some kind of weary girl-queen sitting across the table from me. A princess, taken hostage, trying to maintain her dignity—all that thick red hair making her look fierce and fragile at the same time. Maybe, I thought, she was even more gorgeous than Desiree.

Around us there was the scraping sound of cheerleaders pushing their chairs away from their tables, and someone shouted to the dining hall, "Meet with your squads in fifteen minutes!"

When I reached over to pour myself some water from the pitcher on our table, I saw that the other Kristi was crying after all.

"I'm sorry," she said, dragging the back of her hand across her eyes. A tear ran down her face and fell from her upper lip onto her plate, into her potato salad, and it crossed my mind absurdly for a second that it was her tears that had turned the potato salad pink.

"It's okay," I said, and exhaled. "Are you all right?"

"Yeah," she said, but then she began to cry harder.

"You'll be okay," I said. "I have some Pay Days in my duffel bag. If you want to, we can go get one now."

"No," she said, and I noticed over her shoulder that Slippery Lips was looking at us. She didn't have her glasses on and seemed to be squinting to see what was going on. "I'm not hungry," the red-head said.

"You're just homesick," I said. "Another couple days— "

"No." She shook her head violently enough to dislodge her ponytail, and her hair cascaded out of the rubber band and fell around her shoulders. Suddenly, as if by some miracle, the tears completely disappeared, and evaporated so quickly it was as if they'd never been there. When she spoke, her voice was stronger and louder than it had been before, as if she'd had two voices in her all along, as if she'd been saving this one for a special occasion, a more serious voice that came from a deeper place inside her.

"I'm not homesick," she said. "And I'm not hungry. I just know something terrible is going to happen."

I cleared my throat and looked at the ceiling, then looked back across the table at her.

Her face was flushed. I thought that if I put my hand across the table, I would be able to feel her blazing over there like a fire. It was a little scary, all that intensity where a moment ago there'd just been tears and complaints. But she also sounded ridiculous, and I had to press my lips together to keep from laughing when I thought about telling this to Desiree.

(*Something terrible is going to happen,* and those big eyes.)

However sorry I'd felt for Little Miss Frigid only a moment ago, it was gone now. Her eyes were so wide, it was as if a director offstage were holding up saucers and mouthing the word *wider.*

"Is this about the boys?" I asked. "Because—"

"Forget it," she said, shaking her head, more gently this time. "Forget it. Forget I told you. I knew it wouldn't do any good to tell you. It won't do any good to tell anyone."

Then she gave me a tragic little half-smile, shook her head again, this time dismissively, knowingly. She got up from the table and walked straight out of the dining hall.

8

"To the lake!" Desiree had shouted, as we sped out of the gas station and back onto the road.

She reached over and snapped my stereo on, turning it up.

The rusty station wagon disappeared behind us, and Desiree said, "We lost 'em," leaning over my stick shift to look into the rearview mirror. When she did, a strand of her hair flew into my mouth. I tried to spit it out, and we both laughed when I finally managed to push it away, shaking my head and sputtering. Her hair tasted familiar to me, like the wind.

The needle on the speedometer was jerking around between 68 and 70, and the trees blurring by looked soft and solid at the same time, as if we were driving through a tunnel constructed of green sweaters—a blur I could smell. Fresh and festering at the same time. When we passed a sign that said *Lovers' Lake 3 mi,* I said, "That's our lake. We're almost there," and Desiree shouted, "Here we come!"

But we hadn't driven another mile when the redhead in the backseat shouted up at us, "I have to go back to camp. *Now.* I've got my period."

"What?" Desiree said, turning to look at her. "You *what*?"

"I've got my period. I have to go back." The redhead had to lean up between the front seats so we could hear her. When she did, the bandana in her hair slipped down over her face and covered her eyes.

"You don't have any tampons?" Desiree shouted back at her.

"No. I don't have *anything.* Do *you*?"

"Fuck," Desiree said.

I was the only one with a purse, because my purse had been in the trunk of my car when we left, and I knew I had no tampons. I'd had my period the week before. And Desiree herself had only the few things she carried around in a little backpack with her at camp—the blue bandana, some insect repellent, her cigarettes, and a lipstick.

"Shit," I said, and glanced in the rearview mirror. I could see her holding an arm across her lower stomach as if she were in pain. "I guess we're going back," I said, looking at Desiree.

"I guess we are," Desiree said, rolling her eyes. "And we'd even managed to unload your losers."

"Sorry," the redhead called up to us, but she didn't sound sorry. She sounded sarcastic.

Really, it didn't matter very much. We'd only sneaked out on a whim. Lovers' Lake had been an afterthought. Still, once we were on the road, with the deepest lake in the state our destination, swimming in it our goal, I'd started to get excited. I'd imagined the entry in my diary: *Swam today in the state's deepest lake.* I would write it down in purple pen, right under the date.

It was a pink vinyl diary with a little heart-shaped lock—although I'd lost the key and had to pry it open with a butter knife, so now the lock was busted and I had to hide the diary under my mattress to keep it from the eyes of my mother. I wrote everything in it. Each event of my life became a souvenir of itself, and sometimes I wasn't sure whether the things I longed to do were for their own sakes or so I could write them down in my diary, in the same way it was hard to tell which was more important to my stepfather: the event itself or the roll of photos he was hell-bent on taking to record every single second. All those tiny Grand Canyons, the backs of brides' and grooms' heads, the shiny fading leftovers of a well-lived life.

But, *swam today in the state's deepest lake* was going to have to wait. She wasn't joking. I could see that. I didn't like her, but I knew what it was like to get your period when you least expected it. Disaster. Once, during cheerleading tryouts, I was wearing a pair of white shorts when Desiree came over and whispered into my ear so loudly I had flinched: "There's *blood* on your *shorts.*"

I'd run for the locker room, and she'd followed, and I'd sat inside the locked stall for a long time, panicking, while Desiree paced around outside it, trying to reassure me that no one had seen. (There'd been *boys* in the gym, tossing basketballs around and watching the cheerleaders out of the corners of their eyes.) After she'd finally calmed me down, I realized I was trapped in a bathroom stall during the one thing in the world I could not miss—tryouts. "*Now* what?" I'd called to her, but she was gone.

I thought Desiree had abandoned me, and I started to breathe so hard through my mouth, I felt like I was going to faint—but she hadn't. Desiree didn't sit around during disasters. She took care of things. She'd gone into the boys' locker room—despite the fact that there were boys in it—and grabbed a pair of gym shorts out of Joe Maroni's locker. She'd sneaked in there with him twice when they were dating and showered with him while everyone else was obliviously watching a girls' volleyball game in the gym, so she knew where his locker was.

Now, Desiree sighed and sat up straighter in the passenger seat, looking over at me. "Let's go back," she said, shaking her head wearily.

"Okay," I said, slowing down. Behind us, I thought I heard the redhead say, "Thank you," but when I looked in the rearview mirror she was looking out the window with no expression at all on her face. "But it's going to be a minute," I said. "There's no place to turn around here. No shoulder."

And it was more than that.

The road we were driving along had been guarded on both sides with tall pines, but suddenly the gravelly shoulder between the blacktop and those pines disappeared, and the blacktop had edged its way right up to a steep drop-off—a ravine. Now there was nothing left but a thin wall of birch trees. The white pines, which had looked sturdy and regimental, were gone.

These new trees were flimsy with thin trunks that swayed in the breeze, looking skeletal, temporary. Behind them I could see what could only have been Lovers' Lake—a black, empty depth so far below us it was impossible to really see if it was water, or nothing.

"Just flip a U," Desiree said, making a U-turn in the air with her index finger.

"Hell no," I said, looking at both sides of the road.

It was beginning to narrow even further now, and I couldn't see more than a few feet ahead of me, or behind. The line down the center of the road was solid yellow, and there was no way to see what was coming from either direction. To our right, beyond the white peeling trunks of those birches, lay the wrinkled darkness of the state's deepest lake. Sure, I'd wanted to skinny-dip in it, but I definitely did not want to sink to the bottom of it in my little red car.

"Come *on,*" Desiree said. "Flip a U."

She had slouched down again in the passenger's seat and was shaking her head. Whenever Desiree did this, I knew she was losing her patience with me. She'd done it all the way back in kindergarten, standing over me, waiting for me to be done with the blob of paste I'd been given on a square of paper and been told to share with my neighbors. "Come *on,*" she'd say.

One thing I definitely didn't appreciate was when she told me how to drive, even when she was right. Desiree did not even have a driver's license yet, having flunked the driver's exam on her sixteenth birthday. She'd taken the bumper off her father's Buick when the examiner asked her to parallel park between two cop cars, and her father hadn't let her drive since.

I, on the other hand, was a good driver.

Cautious, but not overly so.

I only broke the speed limit when there was no one around, and had never once driven the car over seventy-five miles an hour, not even on the freeway. I always put on my blinker far in advance of changing lanes, and when I came to a stop sign, I never rolled through it, but always came to a complete stop and looked both ways before driving on. In driver's ed, I'd been the only girl who could parallel park.

"Patience," Mr. Nixon had said, gesturing in my direction after the car was safely tucked into its small space. "Kristy Sweetland's success here is due to her *patience*."

But when the other girls tried to be patient, they still ended up in tears instead of parallel parked.

My one weakness was being a little jumpy on the brake. The idea of running over an animal was so appalling to me that I sometimes stepped on the brake or swerved for shadows. Those first few months after I'd gotten my license, even when butterflies or little white moths fluttered into my path, I'd swerve to avoid them—but I learned soon enough that you couldn't anticipate which direction those delicate things (made of paper, air, an afterthought) would blow when you swerved. So I gave up trying, but I always felt bad when it happened. That tissuey little life snuffed out because of me.

Despite the fact that she didn't even have a driver's license, let alone a car, Desiree was *always* giving me advice on how to drive mine. But even though I resented it, I usually took it, simply because I'd been taking Desiree's advice almost all my life.

"*Do* it," she said. "Make a U-turn." And I grumbled, "Oh, okay," not bothering to glance in the rearview mirror because I knew I'd see nothing but the road rising behind me (and tree branches and glare—we were at the bottom of a crest). Ahead of us there was nothing to see except that optical illusion of water evaporating in black veils from the road as soon as you drove close enough to really see it.

"Here we go," I said, and slammed on the brakes, turning the steering wheel hard to the left until I was straddling both lanes and my tires were squealing again. The redhead in the backseat screamed and grabbed Desiree's headrest, her knees braced against the seat.

Then, when we were halfway turned back into the direction from which we'd come, I saw them.

Rising slowly, deliberately, up and over the hill we'd just descended, moving inexorably in our direction in their rusty wagon—the two boys from the Standard Station.

"Shit," Desiree said.

"They're still following us," the redhead announced from the backseat, to which I said, "No kidding."

When I'd completely straightened the car into the right lane, I stepped on the gas, and we lurched forward. The redhead gasped, and Desiree said, "Whoa!" and I felt my heart fly briefly out of my chest and hover outside of the car, the way it did sometimes on roller coaster rides. But then we were completely turned around, headed back where we'd come from, simply speeding along as if we'd always been in this very lane, driving eternally in this direction, accelerating away from Lovers' Lake and back to Pine Ridge Cheerleading Camp.

What, I wondered, would the boys in the station wagon think when they saw us now? Would they think we'd turned around to avoid them—or *for* them? Or would they know we'd never even seen them? Would they guess that our change of plans had nothing at all to do with them?

They'd think all of those things, I supposed,

and they'd have no idea what to think.

We drove in silence for a moment. The station wagon had dipped under a hill, so we couldn't see it, but there was no reason to think it wasn't still headed in our direction.

"Well," Desiree said, raking her hair out of her face with her fingers, smiling. "We might as well make their trip worthwhile. We don't want them to think that Little Miss Smiley Face here's a cock-tease, do we?" She boosted herself up then on the headrest of the passenger seat and quickly pulled her orange top up over her breasts. She threw her head back and let her hair fly out behind her in all of its whipping gold, leaning backward as if she were posing for *Playboy*, laughing into the wind.

"Dez," I said. "Sit down!"

But it was no use.

Her breasts were small, with pointed deep-brown nipples, and although she made fun of herself a lot ("I'm secretary of the Itty-Bitty-Titty Club," she'd say, walking topless around the locker room after cheerleading practice), Desiree loved her breasts and took every opportunity she could to flash them. At a concert once she'd kept her shirt and bra off for so long she'd finally *lost* them, and we'd had to cover her up with paper towels when we left.

"I thought you didn't want to lead them on," I shouted up at her. "*I* wasn't even supposed to fucking *smile*."

"Well, I thought you *did* want to lead them on, you little slut," she shouted down to me. "Besides, they can't do anything now. They're headed in the wrong direction."

And it was true.

They'd never be able to turn around again, to follow us, to catch up now. The narrowness of the road. No shoulder. The width and lethargy of their rusty station wagon.

They were still about a half-mile away, wallowing toward us, stubbornly, stupidly, rising over the hill and then disappearing under it again. They couldn't have seen Desiree and what she was doing yet, and maybe we would pass them so quickly they'd never even really be sure they'd seen what they'd seen at all.

So, I reached behind my neck and undid the knot at the back of my halter top and let it fall away.

The wind surprised me, whipping across my bare breasts, which spent so much time hidden away that it was strange and wonderful to feel the sun, the wind, on them. From the backseat I heard the redhead laugh—a high-pitched cackle that sounded strange coming from her. I had not, I realized in that moment, heard her laugh until then. When I looked in the rearview mirror, I saw that she, like Desiree, was sitting up, balanced on the edge of the backseat with her white T-shirt pulled up to her neck and her bathing suit top in her hand, holding it in the air above her where it snapped like a fluorescent pink flag. Her breasts were bare and blindingly pale in the sunlight. White and soft and blowsy, looking as if they'd been made out of papier-mâché, then coated with talcum, or stardust, or crushed handfuls of spiderweb. The nipples were wide and pink.

The station wagon was only thirty or forty feet away from us now. The sun had made a golden rectangle out of the windshield, which blinded me briefly, and then we were passing each other in opposite directions on either side of a solid yellow line—close enough that the wind between us shook the Mustang and seemed to rock their old station wagon. And when I glanced over I saw, in a brilliant glimpse, the expression on the driver's face.

His mouth was open, his eyes were wide, and I could see that his lips were moving, that he was mouthing the words *oh my God, oh my God.*

I couldn't help it.

I smiled again.

I smiled again, and when I did I saw the gratitude for it on his face—the stunned joy. He was really young. Straggly black hair. That wrinkled Sunday school T-shirt. He must have just gotten his license, if he even had it yet, and gone off for the afternoon in his mother's station wagon, looking for girls. And then, this jackpot, this peek into boy heaven.

He would never catch up, but I'd given him this glimpse of it, and he smiled back.

"So long, suckers!" Desiree yelled as we passed.

When I raised my hand from the steering wheel to wave, they were already gone.

I didn't look in my rearview mirror, but if I had, I would have seen only a radiant emptiness where they'd been.

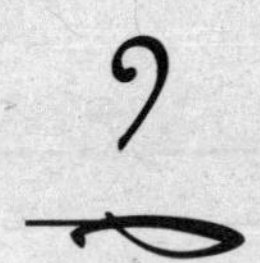

"Desiree," I said, with mock seriousness. "I have bad news. Little Miss Frigid says something *terrible* is going to happen."

"Oh no," Desiree said, putting her hand to her heart and pretending to panic. "Maybe we're *all* going to get our periods, and there *won't be any tampons*."

"Or maybe I'm stuck in a cot next to a mental case who's going to kill me in the middle of the night," I said.

"Are we sure her name is *Kristi*? Maybe it's *Carrie*." Desiree shot her hand up in the air, as if from the grave.

"She's freaking out. She didn't even take her potato salad with her when she got up from the table," I said. "I had to scrape her plate."

"Well, shit, Kristy, that seems only fair. I mean, with her extrasensory perception she can't be expected to bus her own table, *too.*"

"True," I said. "She claims those boys from the gas station followed us here—"

"Hey!"

We both closed our mouths and turned around. It was Mary Beth Brummler, our squad leader, and she had her hands on her hips. "We can't very well get a routine together with you two over there *chatting*, can we?"

"No, sir!" Desiree said, turning and saluting.

"Sorry," I said.

We shuffled over, took our places in line, and listened to Mary Beth Brummler talk about the benefits and liabilities of having a dance routine rather than a precision routine. It was clear that she herself was against the dance routine, and we all knew it was because she couldn't dance—but we had to listen to her anyway because she was our captain.

As Mary Beth talked, she twirled her strawberry-blond hair around and around her finger. When another girl would speak up and Mary Beth had to be quiet for a moment, she'd put the hair in her mouth and chew on it—a habit I myself had broken after my mother told me about a teenage girl who'd had stomach pains and when they operated on her they found a five-pound hairball in there. I could never shake the image of it—that soft drenched thing being pulled out of you like a baby or a squirrel's nest.

Mary Beth Brummler was, perhaps, the only girl at East Grand Rapids High School who was more despised than Desiree. She was pretty and rich, and the other slightly less pretty, less rich girls couldn't stand it. A rumor had started up freshman year that some older girls, driven mad with jealousy over Mary Beth Brummler's strawberry-blond hair, were planning to ambush her outside the gym some afternoon after cheerleading practice and shave her head.

But they never did. They never liked her (*Fuck MBB* was scrawled in permanent marker in every volume of the World Book encyclopedia in the school library), but after a few weeks of having her at the high school they must have realized that Mary Beth Brummler, despite her beauty, held only the most distant interest for boys and that this would never change. She couldn't be sexy or mysterious because she never shut up. She walked into class talking, walked out talking, talked in the hallway, answered all the questions in class, talked through study hall, talked through assemblies, and left school talking and shouting to her friends, "I'll call you when I get home!"

When they saw her coming in their direction, boys fled. Desiree called her Mary Beth Babbler. "She of the diarrhea of the mouth."

Mary Beth went on and on, and when the sky had finally darkened to the color of a new bruise, the cicadas suddenly switched themselves off, and Mary Beth miraculously closed her mouth, and we all looked at the same time up at the sky.

Where had they gone?

How had they known, all together, to stop?

It was dizzying, the sudden return to silence. We'd forgotten that the sound of them was not, itself, a kind of silence, so it was as if all around us some new level of nothing had been achieved. For a moment, no one said a word, as if we, too, had been switched off. We just stood and stared at the emptiness overhead for a moment, and then turned back to the task of planning the routine as if nothing had happened. No one mentioned the cicadas. But Desiree turned to me and said, "This is a total waste of time. Let's get the hell out of here." She cleared her throat then and announced to the rest of our squad, "We're done. I have to go to the bathroom," and began to walk away. Over her shoulder she said, "Follow me. I have to tell you something. Let's go to the girls' room."

But when we got there, although the stalls were empty, it was impossible to stay and talk because it smelled so powerfully of sewage—deeply rank and old. It was as if a decade of cheerleader-waste was seeping up through the earth after having festered under there through so many winters and summers it had changed into something that almost smelled sweet.

"Jesus," I said.

Desiree put a hand over her mouth and nose and walked back out the door. "We can't talk in there," she said. "Let's go to my cabin."

The sun had begun to set, and the pine trees cast such long shadows across the path that I stumbled once or twice, hesitating before stepping onto them because they looked like holes in the ground, and I was afraid to fall in. Desiree stepped lightly over those shadows, seeming not to notice, and she stood outside the door of her cabin waiting for me.

When she opened it, I could see that her empty cabin was an exact replica of my own—four cots on one side, four on the other, each cot containing an empty sleeping bag, windowsills crowded with the same paraphernalia as mine—shampoo bottles, brushes, tubes of Clearasil.

Behind us, the door slammed, and Desiree sat down on her cot. I recognized her sleeping bag and the damp Barbie beachtowel tossed over the windowsill, and I stood at the foot of it looking down at her, waiting to hear what she had to say, assuming it had something to do with T.J.—sneaking out with him, having sex with him, talking him into breaking up with his girlfriend, if he had one. But Desiree cleared her throat, looked up at me, and said, "She's not *completely* nuts."

"Who?" I asked.

"Little Miss Frigid."

"What do you mean?"

"She *did* see those guys. I saw them too."

"What?" I said, taking a step backward, shaking my head. "What are you talking about, Dez? There is *no way.*"

"Sorry, Little Miss Smiley Face. I hate to break it to you, but there *is* a way. While I was walking ahead of everybody else, back to the cabin after Free Swim, I saw them. They were off in the woods—but I saw the one guy's cap. It was orange. And the driver, his plaid shirt. I know it was them. When they realized I could see them, they took off running."

I sat down on the cot opposite Desiree's.

I shook my head.

"Dez," I said. "It's impossible. I mean, I believe you saw some guys in the woods, maybe, but not *those* guys. How would they know—?"

And then I remembered.

The cashier at the Standard Station.

The one with the gray tooth.

He'd asked where we were going, and I'd said Lovers' Lake. He'd asked where from, and I'd said Pine Ridge Cheerleading Camp. After we flashed the boys, after they lost us, they could have gone back to the gas station, I realized, they could have asked that guy if he knew where we were headed, and he knew because I'd told him.

"Who knows?" Desiree shrugged. "Anyway. We've got company. Thanks to you."

"Oh, *come on,*" I said, standing up, sounding more angry and defensive than I'd meant to sound. I realized that my heart was beating hard and that my palms were cold and wet. I lowered my voice and said, "It was *your* idea to flash them, Desiree."

"Yeah," she said, and huffed a little out of her nose, standing up too. "But you're the one who smiled in the first place. They wouldn't have followed us if you hadn't smiled."

Desiree was smiling herself, at me, but I could see that she was serious, and that she blamed me. "Don't worry," she said, patting my shoulder. "They'll get bored, or arrested, or something. Or we can sic T.J. on them. Nothing *terrible* will happen."

The darkness that sank over Pine Ridge Cheerleading Camp after the sun set was so absolute that I felt as if I could have scooped it out of the air with my hands. It would be rubbery, liquid, but so thick it would be impossible to ever wash it off.

This was nothing like the night sky over East Grand Rapids, which leaked light from every edge of the horizon.

It was never so dark at home, even in a closet, that you couldn't see your hand in front of your face, or that, if you had the rest of your life to do it, you could have actually counted every star in the sky.

In East Grand Rapids, they were just a smear,

the stars. And I'd forgotten, from the year before, the way the stars here over the Blanc Coeur National Forest blinked on one by one until they were a shimmering of pinpricks overhead—looking fizzy, carbonated, like an ocean of 7-Up spilled all over the black sky, each individual bubble illuminated from within.

But they didn't help you see, those stars.

They made the darkness even more disorienting, like the campfire, which was so hot and bright and orange-red that it only blinded me more completely. It blazed up from the pile of logs in searing tongues that left me blinking black stripes, and then sank down into itself in deep-blue pockets. It had turned the other cheerleaders to black silhouettes, so I was no longer sure who the girl next to me was. Her face, *all* the faces, were blacked out by fire and night. All I could see were legs and shoes in the dust, and I couldn't see Desiree at all. She was probably on the other side of the campfire with T.J.

No one was talking.

One of the counselors had just finished telling a story about a girl who'd woken up in the middle of the night when her dog licked her face, but when she got up, she found her dog with its throat slashed in the bathtub:

So, *who or what had licked her face?*

There were groans when the story was over, and someone said, "I don't want to hear *any more.*" And then another one of the counselors said, "Really. We've all got to get a good night's sleep tonight. No more stories."

So, now there was a silence among us which had allowed the sound of the bonfire to take over—a slow, rolling roar. It was impossible not to stare at it, not to listen to it—even though I had a feeling that, like the sun, my mother would have warned me not to look directly into it, that staring right at it and listening to it too long might damage me forever.

But despite my mother's warnings, I would sometimes sneak a peek, even at the sun. I knew it could burn my eyes out, burn its way straight into the back of my brain and singe the nerves there that made it possible to see the world in anything more than black outlines—but I did it anyway. I'd be lying on a towel in the backyard in my bikini, the radio next to my face making a fuzzy attempt at music, with a paperback book, its covers curled up from tanning oil. I could smell my own flesh baking as the sun pushed heavily against my eyelids—a huge burning force in the sky, and I'd have the urge to see it. I'd open my eyes just a little and peek at it through the veil of my eyelashes until a little window of tears grew between me and the sun. Then, I might open my eyes wide and take it all in, a terrible flash, before closing them tightly again.

"Our little sun worshipper," my stepfather would say as he walked from the back door to the garage. "Are we beseeching Ra for the perfect tan?"

My stepfather collected Egyptian things. It had become his hobby when he got rich. Our house was full of small engraved sacred objects made out of clay, shelved behind glass. It was an extensive collection, and Egyptologists would come to the house regularly to examine it. Occasionally they too would say hello as they came and went from the house while I sunbathed in the backyard.

I'd say hello back, without bothering to look up.

Most of his objects were shards and fragments, but my stepfather also owned the mummified remains of a cat, a falcon, and a human being.

These things were behind glass in his study—and although the cat and the falcon just looked like lumps wrapped in rags, the human being still looked like a human being.

We always referred to that mummy as *him,* and sometimes we gave him names: Dudley. Gomer. Rupert.

He was no larger than a ten year old, but that could have been because he'd shrunk with time and decay or because people had been smaller back then. Less protein. Bad genes. He was wrapped in thick brown strips of something rough and dry, but here and there it had torn away enough to reveal what looked, inside, like a dusty piece of beef jerky. The skull seemed to have fallen in on itself, and underneath the strips were hollow places and sharp pieces of bone where once there'd been a face. Smiling. Crying.

Once, that mummy had been able to make expressions.

Terror. Disgust.

It had flirted. It had been loved.

But now it was just an object, a curiosity, something that wasn't exactly dead because it was hard to believe it had ever been alive.

Dudley. Gomer. Rupert.

None of those could have been its name, we knew. Still, it came as a surprise, long after we'd grown used to thinking of the mummy as a shrunken man or an old boy, when the Egyptologists X-rayed it and said they were pretty sure the mummy was a female, probably prepubescent, some kind of servant to royalty. She had certain skeletal attributes—her ribs, her pelvis, her femoral bones—which seemed to indicate she'd been a young girl when she died. And the bit of clothing fiber they were able to analyze was woven in a manner common to the clothes worn by the rich. She'd probably been laid in the grave right next to her dead master and buried when he died, although she herself would have still been alive. Now she was in my stepfather's study in a glass box.

A kind of awful Snow White.

A Snow White who'd dried and moldered.

No prince would have kissed that.

My stepfather was right:

It *did* feel like sun worship, tanning in the backyard.

With my eyes closed but my gaze held up to that enormous burning globe, I could hear my own heartbeat (*I am, I am*) and could feel the sweat at my pulse points, the way the water inside my body boiled before it rose to the surface and evaporated. "You're going to be a wrinkled-up old lady with skin cancer," my mother would warn me, as I stood in front of the full-length mirror in the hallway looking over my shoulder to study my tan lines. "Your skin will be leather by the time you're forty."

But we both knew I didn't care. It didn't matter.

Forty? Who ever imagined I'd someday be *forty*?

I was seventeen, with a perfect tan.

Except for the campfire and the smoky smear of stars overhead, there was no sign that there had ever been a sun to worship. If there had been, where was it now? On the other side of the world? Was it shining on China now? Rising already on Siberia? Were there reindeer there, grazing while the sun smoothed itself pinkly over the east, like something radioactive that had been slipped into a balloon and sent into the sky?

Or maybe now the sun was at high noon and beating down on the sphinx, pouring itself sandy and yellow onto its huge paws.

At home in East Grand Rapids, it was, of course, night, just as it was here. My bed there would be empty except for a few stuffed animals lined up against my pillows. Outside my bedroom window, the long rolling lawn would look like black wall-to-wall carpeting, and the one enormous tree at the center of it would look like a dark leafy brain. The shelf on the wall above my bed would be collecting dust on its kitten bookends, propping up a line of paperbacks between them: *A Separate Peace, Jonathan Livingston Seagull, A Wrinkle in Time, Lord of the Flies.*

It was hard to picture my bedroom without me in it, just as it was hard to imagine the world if I'd never been born to see it. When the sun rose over my stuff, I wouldn't be there to witness it, unlike most summer mornings, when I woke up in my own bedroom slowly, long after it had already risen and was shining through the cracks behind my window shades.

For a while, I'd lie on my back and watch the model of the solar system, which I'd tacked above my bed. It moved listlessly in the still air.

It was just a flimsy model of the solar system that someone's older brother had made as a high school science project many years before. The planets were hopelessly off-scale (Mars being, for starters, twice, rather than half, the size of the

Earth). He couldn't have gotten more than a C.

Years later it fell into the hands of a senior at East High, who gave it to the senior class president, who passed it on to me at the Senior Wills assembly.

Every year the seniors willed things to the juniors. The best senior on the baseball team might will his glove to the best junior. The captain of the girls' swim team might pass on her swim cap to the future captain.

But there were joke wills, too.

A senior boy might will the sex appeal of the sexiest senior girl to the sexiest junior.

Someone might will a hand mirror to a junior girl known to be vain.

Desiree had been willed a paper fan, "to cool her off."

But it was in good fun.

The seniors were leaving. They had no more axes to grind. Whatever was willed might poke fun at you, but it was never intended to hurt. For mine, Sean Burns, president of the senior class, brought the mobile up to the podium.

"To Kristy Sweetland," he said, holding it up, "we will this model of the solar system, so she can see that the world revolves around the sun, not her."

There was laughter and stomping in the bleachers and a chant of my name as I walked onto the gym floor to take it from him. I sprinted, waved, smiled. I took it from him and held it up. And then I took it home and tacked it to the ceiling above my bed.

I loved it. It was just a careless teenage kid's class project, but there was an elegance to the way those Styrofoam balls circled one another smoothly, hanging off a wire coat hanger from strands of fishing line—strands that were invisible in most light but, particularly so in the morning light of the sun through drawn window shades, so that when I first woke up it appeared to me that the planets were truly afloat.

Some mornings, if I were in the mood to hear it, that elegance almost seemed to produce a palpable music—a music I felt and heard at the same time, like breath being blown into a glass bottle, or a sharp silver knife being drawn slowly across the rim of a crystal bowl. But airier, more diffuse, a million times stranger and more beautiful.

I was not the center of the universe.

But also, I was.

The Earth revolved around the sun, not me.

But none of it would have existed if I hadn't been there to see it.

That model of the solar system, without me in my bed in the morning watching—that universe would revolve around nothing at all.

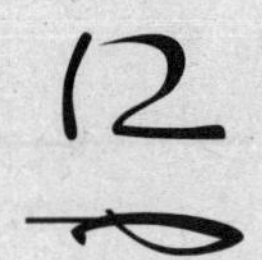

The cheerleader beside me, whoever she was, had fallen asleep.

Over the sound of the campfire, I could hear the regular in-and-out of her breath.

But how could she, sitting like that on a log with a fire only inches from her feet, have dozed off? When I looked over at her, I saw nothing but a black shadow in a hooded sweatshirt. When I looked back to the center of the campfire, I could see things deep inside curling up—birch bark, newspaper, a magazine, rifled through by the fire, each page blackened as it was turned, then disappearing.

Seventeen, I imagined.

Or an old issue of *Boy's Life* that had belonged

to T.J., who'd built the fire for us earlier as we sat around him in a circle, when the sun was still giving up a last bit of light, so he could see to construct a flammable tent out of long dry branches, stuffing it with crumpled newspaper.

There was giggling and chatter as T.J. tossed the magazines in and threw some burning matchsticks into the center of that tent—but mostly we were watching him.

It was impossible not to.

When he leaned over, his Falcons jersey crept up his back so that we could see his skin—deeply tanned, smooth, covered with a fine, blond down.

When he stood up, his stomach muscles were visible underneath the thin cotton—so solid-looking it seemed that he was made of marble.

He was taking his job of building a campfire seriously and seemed to be paying no attention at all to the twenty-seven pairs of eyes (and the counselors', who were watching him too) following him as he broke sticks over his knee, and tossed those magazines into the pile.

Boys were always most beautiful when they were busy at their work, oblivious to the girls. Sweating on a basketball court. Running down the football field with a ball. If they knew we were there, screaming ("Hornets, hornets, take the heat. We've got the boys who can't be beat!"), it was impossible to tell.

Girls, on the other hand, were most beautiful when they were strutting, posing, on display.

All those Miss Americas lined up and smiling.

Clearly, someone had told each and every one of them to look directly into the camera when they answered the question, "What would you do to improve the world if you could?"

"In my world, no child would ever go hungry," they'd each say, unblinking, with those smiles turned right on that perfect world—a world I pictured like something my mother would have beaten out of egg whites. Pure and white, but also stiff to the touch.

Those contestants were expected to smile blankly and equally at everyone who looked at them if they wanted to be lovely—but boys *did* stuff, and ignored everyone. Like T.J., building that fire. His hair had gotten messy, and there was a damp spot of sweat between his shoulder blades, and although we pretended not to be, we were riveted. Only Desiree was able to take him in casually, leaning back on her elbows, watching in silence with a secret little smile on her face.

When I'd stared at the campfire long enough, I began to see shapes at the center of it—figures, shadows—as if the pages of those magazines were releasing their contents to the sky as they burned.

Limbs, hair, bridal veils.

Pom-poms. A Boy Scout with a fishing pole. A girl on a bicycle.

The fire let them go, released them from their forms in the substance of smoke.

I watched them swirl upward until someone shouted, "Okay, girls!" and for a moment I wasn't sure if the voice had just startled me or actually woken me up. "A great second day! Let's get some sleep so we can have a great third day! Back to the cabins!"

We all stood in unison then and turned toward the path to file back to our cabins, but it was impossible to see where we were going, even with the light of the campfire behind us. We began to grope away from the fire—reaching out for an arm, a tree trunk, some girl's back to show us which way to go.

I got ahold of some girl's shoulder and kept my hand on it, following her, although I had no idea who she was. All I could see was a ponytail. It could have been anyone. It could have been me. My own hair was pulled up now in a rubber band. I could have been following my*self* into the darkness, thinking I was someone else.

Except that she was so solid.

Whoever she was, her shoulder was bony and real.

But the sense of walking without knowing where I started and where I ended, where everyone else ended and began, made me feel anxious. It reminded me of the disorientation of a fun house I'd walked through once at a fair. You passed through a hall of mirrors to find a mechanical clown with a big red smile and a chalk-white face staring into space. His hand moved up and down and a taped loop of a laugh went on and on from somewhere behind him. You would see yourself in a mirror and mistake yourself for someone else. Or you would fail to see yourself and smack right into that rigid reflection of no one. I was remembering that dizzy panic, how *not* fun that fun house was, the mechanical clown getting such a kick out of my stupidity and confusion, when I *heard* it out in the woods.

Somewhere, off the path, a high, cold cackle.

But this time it didn't sound taped.

It sounded real, and close.

Ha-ha-ha, ha-ha.

An ascending scale of what might have been either alarm or satisfaction. There were gasps from the cheerleaders and a moment of hesitation in our progress down the path. "Just a screech owl," someone said.

Slippery Lips.

We began to walk a little faster, and I stumbled on a tree root into the girl in front of me, and she lurched forward into the girl in front of her, who said, "Jesus Christ."

"Sorry," I said, and someone soft-voiced said, "It's okay." I felt grateful to her, and wanted to know who she was, but there was no way to tell. All around me, nothing but shadows and shuffling.

Then, it happened again.

Ha-ha-ha-ha-ha-ha.

Gasps, faltering. Someone else stumbled into the cheerleader in front of her, who said, "Shit."

Screech owl.

"What *was* that?" a girl asked, sounding panicked. Apparently she hadn't heard Slippery Lips the first time, and this time Slippery Lips didn't bother to answer. "Nothing," someone else said.

"That was definitely *something,*" the girl said in a high, scared voice.

"Shut up," someone else said. A familiar voice. Desiree?

Then Slippery Lips spoke up, wearily this time, and said, "It was a screech owl."

"Fuck," the panicked girl said. "I *hate* owls."

"Oh, come on." This time I was sure the voice was Desiree's. She was near the head of the line. "What have owls," she asked, "ever done to you?"

"An owl ate my kitten," another girl said, but she laughed as she said it.

"Yeah, right. You wouldn't know an owl if it bit you on the ass," someone else, not Desiree, said.

"Hey, I saw an owl once at the zoo."

"Did it eat your pussy too?"

Desiree.

We were all laughing now, and the screech owl in the distance laughed with us. *Ha-ha-ha-ha-ha.* I could picture it perched on a tree branch, looking down.

Contempt? Annoyance?

Or maybe that owl was intrigued. What were these girls doing out here in the woods? it wondered. All these girls, tripping through the dark.

That owl would be turning its feathered head around and around on its body to watch us.

I was relieved when we finally reached the end of the path, and glad this time to get to the girls' room and smell the chemical flowers, the pink soap, the reek of sewage underneath.

I used the toilet and hurried back to the cabin to sleep.

But I couldn't sleep.

It was amazing how loud the night was. I could hear moths softly tossing themselves against the window screens, and other things—animals light-footed in the forest, tiptoeing through the pine needles and mulch, moving between the trees, making their secret midnight missions.

And heavier steps out there too.

Bears? Coyotes? Wolves?

And there was a smell drifting through the screens, coming from the woods, too—a smell of rot, decay, something out there that had moldered—and I remembered that pig's head on a stake from *Lord of the Flies,* how it was swarmed with black flies, just as we'd been swarmed by them that afternoon running back down the path from the Free Swim lake.

I propped myself up on my elbows, looking around at the stillness of the cabin.

Could everyone else really all be asleep?

Between the cots, there were electric-blue shadows crisscrossing each other on the floor, cast by moonlight, the color of television static. The moon was big and bright in the sky, having fully emerged from the clouds, a full, fat zero now. When the breeze moved the branches, the shadows moved, too. Watching them, I realized for what might have been the first time in my life that shadows weren't really *anything*—that they were just dark places where there was no light.

An absence, not a presence.

Still, these blue shadows *seemed* to be made of something, something more real than the moonlight that made them. They seemed to be made of energy—but energy you could see, touch, like television fuzz, radio static, fading electrical signals.

The red-haired Kristi, in the cot beside mine, was utterly silent. She hadn't even rolled over or sighed once so far in the night. And the other cheerleaders were also so soundly asleep that, except for the still forms inside their sleeping bags, it would have been possible to believe that they weren't there, that I was the only girl in the cabin.

For a short time, I drifted into what must have been a very shallow dream—a dream in which I was still awake but watching my grandmother at the stove in her kitchen in Indiana. She was making dinner, holding a live fish down in a kettle of boiling water. She was up to her elbows in that boiling pot of water, and I was standing back, amazed, wondering how it was that she could manage this without being scalded. Then she turned from the stove to look at me with a peaceful sleepy smile on her face, and the fish screamed.

I opened my eyes and stared at the cabin ceiling.

When it screamed again, I realized that it hadn't been a fish, or a dream.

It screamed again, and again, and I sat up in my cot.

Whatever was screaming was far away, but loud. Something hysterical deep in the national forest. I held my breath and listened for it again, but it didn't come, and then a voice a few cots over said, "Just a rabbit. They scream when they die. Go back to sleep."

Slippery Lips.

Jesus Christ. She never quit. Even in her sleep she was giving lectures.

A *rabbit*?

How, I wanted to ask her, did she know *that*? Since when was it common knowledge that rabbits screamed when they died? I wanted to whisper these questions to her, but I could see, among the electric-blue shadows, that she'd already burrowed back down into her sleeping bag, so I lay back down too.

Now, however, my pillow felt cold and damp, so I propped myself back up on my elbows again.

It was awful to consider—that small furred thing out there screaming. That fluffy silence that had never so much as whimpered in its life suddenly screaming the moment it was over. How strange it would be to have been voiceless for an entire lifetime only to realize at the last second that all along you'd been harboring this wild cry—nothing at all like the voice you'd imagined you might have, a voice you'd thought would be nothing more than a rabbity and breathy politeness stuffed inside you.

Instead, you'd been home to the screech of a banshee, the shriek of a chased girl caught by her braid and yanked to the ground by a stranger.

I lay back down, but I knew by then that I wasn't going to get back to sleep. I didn't even bother to close my eyes. I listened for the other Kristi's breathing beside me, but there was nothing there—or, if there was, I couldn't hear it. And then, sighing, I realized that, naturally, I'd been assigned to the cabin farthest from the girls' room. I was going to have to get up and go to it whether I wanted to or not, because I had to pee.

The cabin door made no sound opening, and when I stepped outside, I found myself surrounded in one dark swoop by night—pure darkness, nothing but that semi-veiled moonlight up the path to the girls' room. And, except for that moonlight and the phosphorescent light outside the girls' room, in every direction for a hundred miles I could have walked into it (the night, the forest) and found nothing.

There was nothing to find.

That's why, I realized, he'd named it the White Heart.

At the center, it was just more emptiness.

I didn't think about the two drowned girls.

Michi-Wa-Ka.

I hadn't thought about them in years, and I wasn't going to think about them now, stumbling down another path in the middle of the night again on my way to a girls' room. When a memory of the story began to rise to the surface (maybe a glimpse of hair, softly floating in lake water) I pushed it back down, but I started to run anyway, although I could only run so fast in the dark in my flip-flops.

I had almost reached the bottom of the path—had already gotten close enough to the girls' room that I could see how the cinder block glowed in the phosphorescence, that the door was propped open with a wedge of wood, and that moths were tossing themselves into the light, bumping backward, steadying themselves to try it again—when something off the path, something among the trees, moved.

I stopped.

I wanted to run, but I couldn't move my legs. Something that was and wasn't me—some instinct, some second self—was refusing to let me move a muscle or even to breathe, so I just stood there.

And then it thrashed against some low tree limbs.

And then it sighed.

And I knew then that, unlike that rabbit, no matter what happened next, I would not be able to scream. If it lunged at me, if it came at me with its claws, if it sank its teeth into my thigh or shoulder, I would still be standing there in perfect silence, not a sound would come out of me, because there was no sound in there to come out.

And then I heard it clear its throat.

Then, it giggled.

And I saw it in the shadows.

Desiree.

Desiree and T.J.

"Jesus Christ," I said, trying to catch my breath. I'd put my hands to my chest but couldn't even feel my heart beating in there, as if it had stopped and not yet started again. "What the hell are you doing out here?"

"Nothing," Desiree said, stepping out of the shadows, smiling, shrugging. She was wearing a long T-shirt, a Barbie thing she slept in. Her feet were bare. Behind her, T.J. had his back turned to me. He was shirtless, and, it seemed, he was zipping up his pants.

"What are you doing out here?" I asked again—

angrily, and stupidly, because it was obvious.

"Communing with nature," Desiree said.

"What if your counselor notices you're gone?"

"What if *your* counselor notices *you're* gone?"

"I just came down here to pee."

"So did I," she said.

T.J. turned around then, and although he was in the shadows I could see the one dimple at the side of his smile and that shark's tooth glowing against the tan skin over his collar bone.

"Well," I said to Desiree, "I'll see you in the morning, I guess."

"Night-night," she said, fluttering the tips of her fingers at me.

From inside the girls' room I could hear them crunching together farther into the forest.

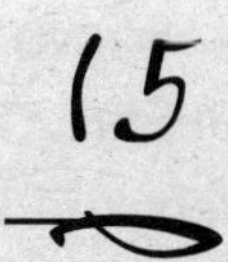

15

Inside the girls' room, the radiance of the fluorescent lights was staggering. I blinked in it, feeling spotlit. I had to hold my hands to my eyes and watch my feet on the floor in order to see where I was going. I cast no shadow on the floor at all.

It took me a moment after peeing, wiping, pulling my panties back up, to hear, under the buzzing and over the sound of my heart and my breath, the sound of something in the stall beside mine.

I'd thought I was alone.

But I was wrong.

The thick white paint on the flimsy metal partition was peeling off to reveal darker shades of white beneath it. And there was someone on the other side of it.

Someone who was trying not to be heard.

"Who are you?" I said, as loudly as I could. "Who's over there?"

Nothing, but I could hear that, whoever it was, was trying not to laugh, and it was causing quick gasps and pants. I stepped out of my stall and, without thinking of what I was doing, pushed the door to that stall open so fast and hard that the flimsy lock on it simply snapped off. There were two of them, balanced barefoot together on the lid of the toilet, holding onto each other's arms. They burst into laughter.

"Fuck you!" I said, and one of them (the stocky girl, the one who'd called Desiree a slut on the path back from the Free Swim lake) slipped off the toilet lid and fell backward against the metal partition, gasping with laughter. Then, the other one, a girl I'd noticed but not spoken to, a girl with short orange hair which she'd straightened so that it looked dry and breakable and stood out from her face, said, to me, "Fuck *you*."

They were both wearing oversized T-shirts

and their legs were bare. Thick. The stocky girl's were hairy.

"Hey," the stocky girl said, "speaking of fucking, looks like your friend is getting fucked out there in the woods. Before you got down here they were doing it doggy style."

The windows near the ceiling. They had been standing on the toilet seat to watch Desiree and T.J. from that stall.

The girl with the orange hair howled like a dog then, and the stocky girl doubled over, crossing her legs to keep herself from peeing her pants as she laughed.

"Go to hell," I said. "How did you ugly bitches get to be cheerleaders?"

This caused them to scream with laughter, which I could hear all the way up the path back to my cabin after I left.

By morning, the blue shadows of the moonlight had been replaced by long pink pillars of sun. Filtered through the pine needles and the cabin's screens, they crisscrossed one another over the cots of sleeping cheerleaders and bled fuzzily at the edges with dust.

They looked substantial, made of only sunlight and dust.

Those pink pillars seemed to be holding up the roof over us.

It was cool and dewy in the cabin, and the forest was still quiet on the other side of the screens—just, now and then, a single bird cry. Beyond that there was nothing other than the sound of breeze skimming over hundreds of miles of trees.

When I'd finally gotten back to the cabin from the girls' room, I'd fallen asleep deeply and slept through the whole night. I'd had a dream that I was given the lead in the school musical, but that I had to cut off all my hair for the role. I was weeping, holding onto my hair the way the other Kristi had held onto hers in the backseat of my convertible, and I was begging to be allowed to wear a wig. But Mrs. Roy, the musical director, kept saying, "The lead or the hair, the lead or the hair, which one do you want more?"

But I wanted them both, and woke up distressed.

I watched the pink pillars shift a little under the weight of sun and dust and remembered that it was the Fourth of July. There would be a picnic, they'd told us, that evening at Vet's Park on Lovers' Lake. Fireworks. We'd wear red, white, and blue and light sparklers after dark. I'd packed an outfit for the occasion. Blue shorts and a red-and-white tube top.

And then it began again.

I'd almost forgotten about it—that long dull electric-drill surge of a voice outside the cabin: the first cicada of the morning, buzzing at me as it held on to the screen. "Christ," I said, and looked over at the cot beside me. "Not again," I said to the other Kristi before I saw that her cot was empty. In a few moments it had flown off, but the others had taken up his scream.

Slippery Lips unzipped her sleeping bag then and stood up, stretching. She'd told us, our first morning, about the value of stretching. How it prevented injury by lengthening and warming the muscles. She'd shown us how to do a deep lunge with your legs spread far apart, knees bent, before you did the splits. After the lunge, she'd swiveled and slid straight down the floor with such swiftness that it seemed as if the floor had moved. Her legs were perfectly straight and flat before and behind her, toes pointed, arms in a V over her head, her crotch politely kissing the floor's pine boards.

Now, she bent backward with her hands clasped over her head, and kept bending until she'd bent so far backward that her hands touched the cot behind her before she sprang back up.

She saw me watching, and nodded to the cot beside me. *Where is she?* she mouthed, and I shrugged.

Then she walked over to my cot and whispered, "Don't worry. This is it. This should be just about their last day." It took me a moment to realize that she was talking about the cicadas.

Slippery Lips stood at the foot of my cot, pulling a pair of satin gym shorts up over her panties, dancing to get them on. "Can you go check the girls' room?" she asked, nodding toward the other Kristi's cot. "Make sure your friend's okay? I've got to go to a counselor's meeting."

I wanted to protest that the redhead was not my friend, that I couldn't imagine that the redhead had *any* friends, but there seemed to be no point. "Yeah," I said. "After I get dressed, I'll go."

Slippery Lips went back to her cot then and pulled her canvas shoes out from beneath it. She slipped them on and went outside toward the dining hall. I listened as her footsteps were drowned out by the drone of cicadas, and then I swung my legs out of my sleeping bag.

On my bare feet, the cabin floor was cold, and the cool new sun shining through the pine needles lit up the window screen with a glossy mist. It was impossible to tell where the screen itself ended and the world beyond it began, because that blur of the million little squares of screen blended right into the sun, and if I hadn't known the screen was there, I'd have thought there was nothing in those windows but a shivering haze. I might even have considered stepping into it; considered leaving the cabin through that haze so I wouldn't have to close the door behind me.

Three

When I was ten years old, my mother and stepfather took me to Yellowstone Park.

What I remembered most vividly from that trip was riding in the backseat through Nebraska.

"You whined for four hundred miles," my mother told me.

Nebraska had seemed like eternity to me, although it couldn't have spanned more than the length of a day.

But, during that drive, I'd begun to feel that my life in the back of that sedan might go on forever (the sun warming the side of my face, the sound of the tires on warm tar like so many lingering dark kisses), while I stared at the backs of their heads or the hard faces of my own knees. The same whitewashed landmarks blurred by over and over:

A big blank movie screen in a scrubby field.

An enormous crucifix that looked like a mutant telephone pole.

A cow, stiffly staring out from behind a fence.

Mostly, we drove along in silence or my stepfather played a ball game on the radio. We'd run out of things to talk about after the first two days in the car, but at some point in Nebraska my mother pointed to a long expanse of grass and said to my stepfather, "This is where they did their ghost dancing. You know. Where they thought the whites couldn't kill them with bullets because the dancing made them invisible."

Not long after that we stopped at a pink-roofed restaurant, where my stepfather bought me a rabbit's foot key chain when he paid our check at the register.

I'd wanted it, that rabbit's foot, pointing at it, and giving him the lifted-eyebrow look he said was my "little beggar" face.

After he paid for it, my stepfather handed it over to me, and it was fluffy and pink, but under all that softness there was a hard knuckle of bone that made me feel sick to my stomach when I touched it.

Along with that souvenir from the pink-roofed restaurant in Nebraska, I was given a spoonful of soft, pastel dinner mints, which had been fished out of a dish and which, with their chalky sweetness melting between the roof of my mouth and my tongue, I would forever associate with that dead rabbit's foot on a little silver chain, dangling like a scream.

Desiree stepped out of the shower wearing a cloud of steam and a Malibu Barbie beach towel. I recognized the towel, but it took a little longer for the steam to part, before I could be sure the girl wrapped in it was Desiree. I said, "Desiree."

"Hi there, Smiley."

I stepped back so she could walk past. The skin on her back and shoulders was so red it looked as if she'd stepped out of a furnace instead of a shower. I asked her, "Dez, have you seen the redhead? You know, the other Kristi?"

"Our Polar Princess?" she asked. "No. Why?"

At the sink there were two other girls, mouths full of toothpaste, hair plastered down their backs. One of them was Susie Rentz, who'd gone to our school until her parents got divorced and she moved with her mother to the other side of the district line. Back when she was at East Grand Rapids; we'd been friendly, although perhaps not friends, but here at Pine Ridge Cheerleading Camp she pretended not to know anyone from East Grand Rapids. Sometimes I wasn't sure who'd started the pretending, her or us.

"She's not in the cabin. Is that her, in the other shower?"

"No," Desiree said, "that's *the butch.*" She mouthed the last two words.

"The stocky one?" I whispered. "Or the one with orange hair?"

"The fat one," Desiree whispered back.

I wanted to tell her then that I'd seen those girls in the bathroom the night before, watching her. I wondered if they had stayed in the bathroom all night or if they'd been following Desiree around—gone back to the cabin to sleep when she did, gotten up to follow her down to the shower. It seemed like something Desiree should know, but another girl stepped into the bathroom just then, and the rush of cool air from the door blew the fog off Desiree. I could see that her eyes, like her skin, were red.

She must have been up all night with T.J.

It annoyed me.

If the stocky girl and her friend were stalking Desiree, maybe Desiree deserved it. I started to walk away.

"We have to talk," Desiree said, touching my arm with her hot fingers.

I said, "Whatever. Okay," but kept my back turned to her.

"Wait outside for me," she said.

Outside, the cicadas sounded like bad feedback from a satellite—something man-made, dangerous, spilling out from earth into outer space. I remembered, once, being driven through Indiana on my way to spend my week of the summer with my grandmother. At the edge of a cornfield, I'd seen a rocket.

It was long and white and sleek, and seemed to be crackling with sunlight.

"What's that?" I asked my mother, and she said, "A missile silo."

I had no idea what that meant, and I couldn't remember whether I'd asked or what the answer had been if I had, but it seemed like a strange thing to plant in a cornfield, and I couldn't imagine what it would be aiming at—what enemy, pointing straight up into a sky full of cottony clouds and robins over Indiana. But the cicadas seemed, now, to be making the sound a rocket like that might make as it heated itself up to blast into those clouds.

Still, when I looked up, I could see nothing at all attached to the sound.

No rocket, no satellite, not even a jet flying over—just one turkey buzzard flying low, in a slow circle, its sleepy darkness descending, naked-faced as something out of a very bad dream.

Desiree came out of the bathroom in her pink flip-flops and a short blue robe. Her hair was in the Malibu Barbie beach towel. "Look," she said in a low voice to me, leaning toward my ear, although there was no one around to overhear her. "We have a really big problem."

"What?" I asked. I could smell her breath. Minty, but lush, as if I could almost smell T.J. on her lips and tongue.

"Your friends," she said. "Those grubs."

"*Them* again?" I asked, exasperated. I'd almost

forgotten about *them*, about their pathetic attempt to follow us around Pine Ridge Cheerleading Camp.

"Yeah," she said sarcastically. "When T.J. and I were out here last night"—she nodded her head in the direction of the woods—"we saw them. In the forest. They were watching us."

I was about to tell her that they weren't the only ones who'd been watching her and T.J. (*doggy style),* and that maybe she and T.J. should find a better place to fuck. But she leaned in to me and said, "There was a note in my cot. A fucking *note.* I didn't see it until this morning. It said, 'We're watching you.'"

"From who?" I asked.

"Well, nobody signed it, stupid. But it had to be them."

"Oh, please," I said, taking a step away from her. "How would they get into your cabin, Desiree, and even if they did, how would they know it was *your* cot?"

"Yesterday. Before the campfire. They were following us. They saw us in my cabin, talking. Don't you get it, Smiley? These fuckers are *serious.* They're not just going to go away."

"Did you tell anybody about the note?"

"Fuck no. What am I going to say? 'There are these boys my friend encouraged to visit us when we snuck out of camp . . .'"

"Come on," I interrupted her. "It was your idea to flash them, *not mine.*"

"Yeah, well, you were the one who smiled."

"Okay, okay," I said. "So what if they did follow us here? So what if they even put a note in your cot, which I highly doubt? The note probably came from that stocky girl and her friend. They hate your guts, Desiree, and they— "

"It wasn't them."

"What? How do you know?"

"Because they're my friends."

"What?"

"They're my friends, Kristy. After T.J. went back to his cabin last night, I ran into them in the bathroom, and we sat up talking. We made a fire, out at the pit, and smoked, and talked. They're cool. We stayed up all night. We never went to bed."

I could not close my mouth.

Slowly, I shook my head, but I could say nothing.

Desiree took the towel down from on top of her head and began to rub her hair with it. Hard.

If her hair had been dry instead of wet, it might have generated sparks.

"They'll be back," she said. "Today or tomorrow, and they're not afraid. We've got to do something before they do."

"Like what?" I asked. There were girls coming and going from the girls' room now. They didn't look at us.

"T.J. has some friends who are lifeguards at another camp around here. Friends from school. He thinks he and his friends can scare them."

"Why do we need to do that? I mean—"

"Yeah, I forgot. You like them. They didn't put a threatening note in *your* bed."

"Jesus," I said. "I don't believe this."

"Believe it, Smiley. After lunch, we're sneaking out. We're going to find them. Are you coming?"

"No," I said. "I'm not."

"Fine," she said. "You got us into this mess, but I guess it's up to me to get us out, as usual."

Someone touched me on the shoulder then, and I turned around fast. It was the redhead. She was dressed already in gym shorts and a white T-shirt, but her hair was a mess, as if she'd been in the back of a convertible all night instead of asleep in the cot beside me. Her eyes were bloodshot again, and her lips were pale. She said, "Amanda said she'd sent you to look for me. I'm here."

"Oh," I said. "Okay."

"I heard what you were saying," she said, "and Desiree is right. They were here, at the camp, all night. They tried to talk to me."

"What?" Desiree said, and quit rubbing her hair.

"Through the window screen—or, the one in the cap anyway. The other one wouldn't talk. The one in the orange cap said they aren't going to hurt us, that they're just lost."

"Lost?"

I took a step away from her.

For the first time I noticed that she smelled. She smelled like blood, old Kotex, dirty hair. When was the last time she'd taken a shower? What had happened to her Sea Breeze and her Phisoderm and the pink comb she kept in her back pocket? She looked at me straight in the eyes as if daring me to say something about it. Instead, I said, just above a whisper, shaking my head as I said it, "You were dreaming."

"No, I wasn't," she said. "I never slept all night."

"Well, I was in the cot next to you all night, so why didn't you wake me up? Why didn't I hear them if they were talking to you?"

"You were asleep. I was afraid."

"No," I said, shaking my head faster. "That's— "

"Well, did you tell them to leave us the fuck alone?" Desiree asked. Her cheeks had flushed the hot red of her arms when she'd first stepped out of the shower. "Did you tell them to get the hell out of our hair before we get them busted?"

"I didn't say anything," the other Kristi said, walking away. "There's nothing we can say to them now."

The pep coach was wearing a red maternity top, blue shorts, a white ribbon in her hair. She used her megaphone to yell at us: "What do we want?!"

"To win!"

"When do we want it?!"

"Now!"

"What do we want?!"

"Victory!"

"When do we want it?!"

"Now!"

"What do we *want?*

"To *win*!"

"When do *we want it*?"

"*Now!*"

We were shouting, not shrieking, just as she'd coached us.

"Good cheerleaders don't *scream,"* she'd said. "They *call out.* They project their voices from the solar plexus."

She'd pointed to a spot just under and between her breasts and just above the place where her baby was floating around inside her.

When we were done calling out at her from our solar plexuses, the pep coach looked pleased, flushed and smiling. We'd called out so loudly and well that we'd blocked out the sound of the cicadas, and our clear strong voices had echoed against the pine trees and the sky, which was a blue haze just beginning to burn away as the sun rose into it, turning it white.

"*That's* what I wanted to hear," she said into her megaphone. "You can sit down now, girls."

I hadn't realized we were standing. At some point, we'd all risen to our feet, our fists in the air, without being asked to or even noticing that we had. I'd seen it happen to crowds at football and basketball games. I'd cheered at games where old men had been brought to the bleachers in wheelchairs, but stood up finally and stomped their feet.

I'd cheered at games where fights had broken out among spectators on the same side, rooting for the same team. At one game, there had been so much jumping up and down that the bleachers had collapsed—a whole section of fans suddenly yanked onto the ground. Luckily, no one was seriously hurt. But I'd seen it: the way they rose to their feet without knowing they had, without planning to do it, without being aware, even, that they were standing, just something prompted by the way we'd *called out,* as if something contagious had been spread from us to them—our pep—and then swept through them in one wild second.

I'd helped to *make* it happen, but until now, I wasn't sure if it had ever happened to me—that spontaneous rising, that unconscious wholeheartedness.

When I sat back down, the aluminum was cold on my thighs, and I wished I'd worn jeans instead of shorts. My legs were covered suddenly in goose bumps, which my mother always called spookflesh. "Did a rabbit just step on your grave?" she'd ask when I had it, and when I asked her what that meant she just shrugged her shoulders and said it was something her own mother used to say.

I always imagined, when she'd say it, my name on a headstone, and that rabbit, on its way somewhere, pausing briefly over me on the grass.

The pep coach shouted into her megaphone, "*Dedication.* What is it?"

I looked behind me.

A few rows up, the other Kristi was sitting very still, staring down at me with no expression on her face.

Desiree wasn't back for lunch, which was thin slices of pink meat, leaves of lettuce, and bread to make sandwiches. The other Kristi sat down next to me, although I'd sat at the table farthest from the line, hoping she wouldn't see me. Her plate was empty of anything but two lettuce leaves and a thin slice of tomato.

"Hi," she said, and glanced at my plate.

I'd taken six or seven slices of the meat. I was starving. It lay on a piece of bread as I spread mayonnaise on the second slice for my sandwich. "Is she back yet?" she asked me.

"No," I said.

"It's not going to do any good, you know. They're not in town. They're here."

"Right," I said. I lifted the sandwich to my mouth. It smelled sweet. I couldn't help but think of my biology class and that fetal pig, but I bit into it anyway. The salty coolness made me feel as if I might gag, as if I'd French-kissed a dead boy, but I kept eating. If I didn't, I wouldn't have another chance until the picnic at Vet's Park, and by then I'd be so hungry I'd be dizzy, and I might faint. It had happened to me a few times before. Once, in church. Once, singing with the choir in the high school auditorium. I'd passed out and fallen straight backward, right off the top of the risers and onto the floor. "Low blood sugar," my mother said. "You have to take in more calories, and you can't go more than two hours without protein."

"They're not like we thought they were," the redhead said. She hadn't touched her lettuce leaves. She had her hands in her lap, and she was leaning forward, trying to look into my eyes, but I kept mine on my sandwich. "They're quiet. They don't mean any harm."

"Look," I said. "I'm not talking about them anymore. You didn't talk to them through the window screen last night, and if they *have* been hanging out around camp, it's because they're bored."

All I'd seen in St. Sophia in the four summers I'd been through it on my way to and from Pine Ridge Cheerleading Camp was that Standard Station, something called the St. Sophia Casket Company, some small ugly houses, and a convenience store with a banner outside advertising Budweiser and deer jerky, and a sign at the town limits:

WELCOME TO ST. SOPHIA, POP. 2,237, HOME OF THE FIGHTIN' COYOTES

CLASS C TRACK STATE CHAMP

CLASS C SWIM STATE CHAMP

What would there be for the local boys to do in such a place?

I said, "They're hicks. There's nothing to do in St. Sophia in the summer but drive around and look for girls, and sneak around in the woods spying on cheerleaders. You were dreaming when you thought you were talking to them. I was right next to you, and I know you didn't even roll over last night. You need to eat something. You've just got low blood sugar or something."

I picked up my sandwich and continued eating. She said, "Okay," in a patient breezy voice, got up from the table, and pushed in her chair. "I'm not going to Free Swim," she said. "I'm going back to the cabin to lie down. I'll see you at the picnic."

When she was gone, I reached over and took the lettuce leaves and tomato slice off her plate and stuffed them into my sandwich.

The walk down to Free Swim was cooler than it had been the day before, and the cicadas sounded as if they were beginning to loosen their grip on the sky, on their lives. I saw one dead on the ground. Or nearly dead. It was lying on its back, sputtering in the gray dust of the trail as cheerleaders trampled past it in flip-flops, making noises when they saw it. *"Ew. Repulsive."*

Even in its last few moments on earth, it was trying to make that noise, vibrating on the ground.

"Where's your friend?"

I turned around.

It was the stocky girl again. She was wearing a blue one-piece bathing suit, the kind of suit a girl would wear if she were swimming competitively, if she were on a team, not going down to the Free Swim lake to wade and sunbathe.

I realized she did not look masculine, exactly.

She did not look like a boy, but like some kind of bad-tempered animal—a bear that had decided, out of its hatred for girls, to become a girl.

Desiree was the one who'd nicknamed her "Butch," but it didn't fit. She was not really even stocky. She was as long-limbed as all the rest of us, except that she walked hard on the flat soles of her feet. Like a bear. And she kept her shoulders hunched, also like a bear. Her hair was cut short, but it was silky, and if it had been long it might have been curly.

"Suppose she's fucking her boyfriend?"

I narrowed my eyes and noticed that the bear-girl had a dark hair growing out of her neck, long and curled into a C that looked like a pubic hair. I hurried ahead, leaving a space of three or four cheerleaders between us.

I didn't care that she hated Desiree (other girls always had it in for Desiree), but it was disconcerting that Desiree had said, "They're my friends."

It was so unlike Desiree, who was suspicious of everyone, who had *no* friends other than myself or the boys she went out with, if they counted. I tried to imagine Desiree sitting around the fire the night before with those two girls. What would they have talked about? How could they have pretended to *like* her when they *hated* her? But more than that, how could Desiree have fallen for it?

But even this wasn't why I was in such a hurry to get away from her. It was that hair. The hair growing out of her neck. There was something unnatural, or *too* natural, about her—an ugliness that didn't make me feel sorry for her, but made me hate her. She wasn't even ugly. She could have been pretty even. It was as though she knew she could have been wearing a yellow bikini, could have had silky, blown-dry hair, could have painted her nails and passed herself off as one of us—but she'd decided not to. Either because she didn't want to or because it was too hard.

It *was* hard.

I would have been the first to tell her that, yes, it was hard—but it was also necessary.

It took a lot of work, a lot of dedication, to find every stray hair on your neck or knee or under your arms, to spend enough time in front of the mirror every day to be sure that, when you stepped away from it, you would take with you the image you wanted the world to see.

Just keeping *clean* took time.

In junior high I overheard two boys talking

about how girls' crotches smelled like fish. The instant the words drifted over to me, I recalled in one quick flash a commercial I'd seen over and over on television but had never understood. A girl saying to an older woman, "Mom, do you ever get that not-so-fresh-feeling?"

Suddenly, in that moment in the hallway of East Grand Rapids Junior High, I understood what the purpose of that product was, and I had my mother drive me straight to the drugstore after school that day, where I bought a bottle of Summer's Eve.

But the bear-girl had decided it would be easier to be mean. To stay angry. Unattractive. I didn't feel sorry for her. I didn't want to look at her at all.

Because I was walking so fast, I reached the end of the path before anyone else and felt relieved when it opened onto the sandy stretch of beach, and I saw them:

T.J. and Desiree.

They were back already from wherever they'd gone. Desiree, in her blue bikini, was lying at his feet again, and he was wearing his stars-and-stripes bathing suit and had his back to the beach, one arm bent, feeling the muscle of his left bicep with his right hand.

Desiree must have heard the flip-flops on the path, because she propped herself up on her elbows and, using her hand as a visor, scanned the beach until she saw me. Then she stood and dove off the dock, disappearing, and then emerging from the lake with a strand of deep-emerald seaweed around her neck.

I stood on the sand a few feet from the lake and waited for her to wade out.

"Did you find them?" I asked when she was close enough to hear me.

"Yeah," she said. "We saw their fucking station wagon, but they were way ahead of us, and every time we tried to catch up, they disappeared around a corner."

"Oh," I said. It seemed unlikely. Desiree had told me that T.J. drove a black Corvette. How could those boys in the station wagon have stayed so far ahead of that?

"T.J. said it's because they know their way around here and we don't."

"Well, anyway, if they're out driving around, they're not sneaking around camp."

"Yeah," Desiree said. She seemed convinced, relieved.

"Where did you go?"

"Back to the Standard Station. Back down the road we took to Lover's Lake."

"You probably scared them. They won't be back."

"You're right," she said, and I felt relieved too, when she said it. Finally, we were going to forget about the guys from the Standard Station.

"I'll just meet you at the picnic, okay? I'm going to ride over with T.J. He's going to dock a canoe in the reeds at Vet's Park so we can go rowing on the lake after the fireworks, when everybody leaves. Maybe we'll get a chance to go swimming in Lovers' Lake after all."

She raised her eyebrows and smiled as if she were including me.

Was she inviting me along?

It seemed unlikely that T.J. and Desiree would want to take me canoeing and skinny-dipping with them in Lover's Lake. Considering what they'd be wanting to do, they wouldn't be doing it with me along—although it was also true that Desiree had never been too worried about being discreet with her boyfriends. The year before, when my mother and stepfather went to the Caribbean and let me stay in the house by myself, Desiree came over every day with Randy Seuter. She took him into my bedroom, where they stayed for hours. Once, she'd heard me in my bathroom on the other side of the closed door and said, "Kristy, come in here."

I'd opened the door just a crack and peeked in to see Randy Seuter naked, lying on top of my yellow comforter, fast asleep. Desiree was beside him, also naked except for the gold chain she always wore around her neck, something that had been her mother's. Her right arm was under Randy's back. "Can you get me a glass of water?" she asked. "I don't want to move."

I went back to the kitchen and poured the water, but never brought it to her.

I didn't want to get that close to them, like that, on my bed—mostly because I had the feeling that Desiree'd asked for the water in the first place because she wanted me to see her more closely. She wanted me to see her with him.

"Okay," I said. "I'll see you at the picnic."

"See you there," she said.

5

It was amazing to think that if I'd gone to a different high school, if my parents hadn't bought the house on Echo Road, but had bought, instead, a house even one mile farther to the west of Round Lake, on the other side of the invisible line that separated the East Grand Rapids school district from Forest Hills—I'd have had a best friend who was not Desiree.

In kindergarten, I might have met her—a girl named Lisa, or Molly, or Paula. She might have been blond and boy-crazy but she would not have been Desiree. I would know her phone number by heart, the combination to her locker, her favorite song and color and season. I would know what grades she was getting in all of her classes, what percentage points she had to get on the next test in order to get a B-plus or an A.

But this girl, whoever she would have been, was, instead, a total stranger.

She didn't even know I existed.

Perhaps even, at the mall some Saturday, we'd passed each other near the fountain. I would have been walking along beside Desiree, and she would have been with her best friend or boyfriend or sister—best friends in a different life, and not even a whisper passing between us in this one.

And Desiree?

If I *had* gone to Forest Hills High, or if my father hadn't died, or if my mother hadn't married my stepfather, or if I'd never even been born, or if I'd died before Desiree and I had ever met . . .

On my fourth birthday, while my mother wrapped presents for me in the other room, I waited like a big girl in the kitchen for my Pop Tart to come out of the toaster. It was stuck, so I got a butter knife, climbed on to the counter and stuck the knife into that dark slot to get it out, and the next thing I knew I was on the kitchen floor, knocked there by a hot white star that had come crashing out of the kitchen cupboard into my face. "You could have died," my mother had said, crying, holding my face in her lap.

Well, I hadn't, but what if I had?

I knew (or so it seemed) all the girls Desiree might have been best friends with if she hadn't been best friends with me.

Mary Beth Brummler. Amy Goldberg. Laura Black. Allison Salerno. Susie Rentz.

Those girls didn't like her, but it might have been different (*she* might have been different, I supposed) if I weren't there. And there were always beautiful girls who wanted to be best friends with someone even more beautiful than themselves—and there would certainly have been another dozen girls who were maybe a little homely, maybe less popular, maybe not cheerleaders, who might have given anything to be the beautiful blonde's best friend if she didn't already have one.

Still, it was impossible to imagine it:

Desiree sleeping over at the houses of any of those girls. Riding beside them in their cars with her bare feet on their dashboards. Calling them up on a Saturday night *("I did it")*.

It was as if, had it not been for me, there would be no Desiree either.

6

When I got out of my car at the edge of Vet's Park, I could see that T.J. was already there. He was standing behind a barbecue grill with a can of 7-Up in one hand and a pronged fork in the other, turning hot dogs from one side to the other, one at a time. He was wearing a pale blue T-shirt that said LIFEGUARD in big white letters, and his face was flushed, either with sunburn or from the heat that was rising off the grill.

Beyond him I could see the other Kristi sitting by herself at a picnic table looking out at Lovers' Lake.

It wasn't a very wide lake, but its darkness reminded me that it was supposed to be bottomless.

From where I stood beside my car, the lake *did* look bottomless—black, and not a ripple of sunlight shivering on it, it was so still.

Most of the other cheerleaders seemed to have arrived before I did. A few Pine Ridge vans had brought over the ones who didn't have their own cars. I could see Slippery Lips arranging cans in a cooler. And Mary Beth Brummler was doing back bends down by the water, while Amy Goldberg watched. Someone had decorated the picnic shelter with red, white, and blue crêpe paper, and all of the cheerleaders had been asked to wear at least one of the flag's colors. Photographs would be taken, and they'd be pinned up on the wall of the Welcome Cabin. I had on my blue shorts and my red-and-white-striped tube top.

It looked like a flag milling around the edge of Lovers' Lake, in the sand and grass of Vet's Park. In a circle of weeds between the beach and the parking lot there was a huge bronze statue of a weary soldier drinking from a canteen. On his back someone had spray painted FUCK BETSY WALTON. But the red paint had faded to a thinly visible pink. It would make a strange, patriotic photograph for the Welcome Cabin, I thought.

Now, there was no longer any cicada hum at all. It had ended at once in the late afternoon, and no one, not even Slippery Lips, seemed to know if this was because evening was descending or because they were finally dead. But there was no denying that something was different, that they were weakening and falling out of the trees in a gruesome rain—shriveled up, sputtering in the dirt, one by one. It was as if a big switch had been turned off, and they'd all gone silent at once. It was odd to hear birdsong and the rustling of tree branches again.

I finally spied Desiree. She was wearing a red halter top and red shorts, and was standing between the stocky girl and the one with the orange hair. They appeared to be laughing at something she had said. All three had their backs to the lake, so it looked as if a black sheet had been hung behind them. I was just starting toward her when someone behind me, someone with a deep, male voice called out, "Miss?"

I turned around to find a cop sitting in a car that was idling so quietly and so close to me it was as if it weren't a machine but part of him, as if he were half cop and half cop-car.

"Miss?" he asked again, and I stepped over to his blue sedan, smiling.

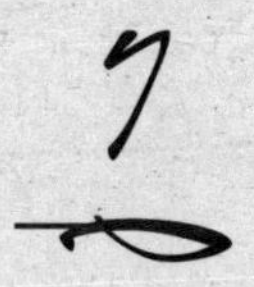

Early on, I'd been told that policemen were my friends, that I could speak to no other stranger, get into no other man's vehicle, but a policeman I could trust. So far, it had always proven itself to be true. They'd always been friendly, soft-spoken, come to our school to tell us what to do if we got lost, what to do if there was a fire, and to tell us never to cross the street without looking (this after Beau McNamara was hit by a car he'd tried to dodge on Lakeside Drive). They reminded us never to take drugs (after a seventh-grade girl was found floating dead in her uncle's swimming pool after taking some pills she'd found on his dresser), and not to stop to talk to anyone passing us in a vehicle on the street. This last lecture came after another girl, in the eighth grade this time, was called over to a white van near the entrance to the junior high, then pulled into the van and never seen again. After that there were policemen outside the junior high and high school every morning for a year, waiting for that white van, which never came back. And although I was two years older than that girl and hadn't known her, I was always happy to see them in their clean cars and blue uniforms. It made it possible to believe that nothing like that could ever happen again, that she was just a particularly unlucky girl.

Still, I thought about her a lot.

Why *her*?

She'd been walking to school with a friend. The friend had stood back when the victim walked over to the white van (smiling politely I imagined). The friend stood on the curb screaming after a man pulled the victim into a van and took off.

Why hadn't he beckoned to the other one?

Or why not *both* girls?

I stared at the photos in the newspaper, but they revealed nothing. The victim's school picture looked ordinary. She had freckles, straight hair that must have been blond but looked gray in newsprint. She was wearing a cowl-neck sweater, and the shadow it cast on her neck looked a bit like a noose. But a million other girls have worn such sweaters for their school pictures, too.

Nothing was the same in East Grand Rapids for a long time. Mothers walked their daughters to school. Teachers asked casually, occasionally, if everyone was feeling safe. Eventually, a policewoman was brought to school to teach self-defense during gym class, just to the girls. She arrived in a green sweat suit on a Friday afternoon and stood in a corner while Mr. Barcheski separated the girls from the boys.

Grimly, the woman in the sweat suit said, "I'm going to teach you some basic self-defense maneuvers, and I expect you to pay close attention."

She positioned herself in front of us with her legs spread and her hands folded in front of her as if she were going to lead us in prayer.

"First," she explained, making her right hand into a claw, "go for the eyes. Use your keys if you have them."

She took her own keys out of her pocket and demonstrated how to lace them through the fingers of the right fist, how to make it look as though you were simply a girl walking down the street, defenseless *(la-la-la),* but look!

She held up the weapon of her hand.

"Who would guess what you could do with something as ordinary as this?" she asked, looking proudly at her own spiked knuckles.

It was good, too, to have a whistle on a rope around your neck to call for help. "Blow it like this," the policewoman said, making a shriek with her whistle that made us all cringe and cover our ears. "Yell, *'Get the hell away from me, you prick!'"*

She made us practice. "I want to hear it!"

"Get the hell away from me, you prick," followed by hysterical laughter.

"This is not a joke," the woman in the sweat suit said, narrowing her eyes so that her face flattened out and she looked like a man-eating fish. "You may need to do this someday, so I want to hear it like you mean it."

"Get the hell away from me, you prick!"

"Again!"

"Get the hell away from me, you prick!"

This time, the chorus was a sober one, and the sound of our war cry rang off the gym walls. The look on the woman's face was serious, but pleased. "That's it," she said, crouching a little with her hands in fists at her side, as if in imitation of a gorilla. "And when you walk down the street, look like you know where you're going, for god's sake. Look like a girl who can kick.

"Look," she said, putting a hand on her hip and tilting her head a bit to the left. She sashayed away from us, swaying her hips, looking suddenly, terrifyingly, like a girl—as if she'd been one once, as if she *were one.*

But it was a caricature, it was supposed to be funny, and it should have made us laugh, but we didn't. She turned around and walked back toward us with her shoulders back, looking straight ahead, walking deliberately, hands in fists at her side, and then she stopped. "Now," she said, "I want you to tell me, if you were a rapist, if you were a murderer, which of those two girls would you go for?"

No one said, or needed to say, anything at all.

And then the lesson moved on to testicles.

A few simple practice kicks on a sandbag held up by a rope in the corner of the gym.

Every girl already knew where *that* soft spot

was. Even the most devoted of stranglers, the policewoman explained, could easily be disabled with a well-placed knee to that area.

She made us practice until we were breathless, doubled over with laughter. Then she stopped us, made us do it over, and this time *feel* the anger.

And then the boys were let back into the gym, red-faced, panting from running laps.

They seemed pathetic, those boys—vulnerable and clueless, blustering around the gym, sweating with confidence and exertion, with those laughable testicles between their legs, no secret, and at our mercy.

Still, after gym class, I felt no more powerful than I had before. I felt pretty sure that, without the protection of the policemen surrounding our school, driving along our streets, I'd be like the other girl, the one she'd pantomimed with her sashay—the girly girl with the smile and the target on her back when the white van pulled over looking for someone to grab. It was luck, and the cops. They would be my friends and my best hope when that white van pulled over.

8

"Is the Mustang yours?" the policeman asked.

He was young but serious looking. He had a handsome face, except he had a birthmark on his cheek, a purplish welt the size of a matchbook, and I could tell he knew it was there, that he knew I was glancing at it too, because he looked away from me, toward my car.

"Yes," I said. "Uh-huh."

"We're looking," he said, and cleared his throat, "for two boys. They were last seen yesterday at a gas station, and a guy who works there said he thought he saw them drive off after some girls in a car like yours."

"Oh," I said, feeling what seemed to be my heart beating on the wrong side of my chest. I put my hand there. I lifted my eyes away from him, pretending to be thinking.

It was something I'd learned to do well in calculus, where we all had the answer book (someone's mother had taught the class as a substitute and had the teacher's edition of our textbook in her basement), and Mr. Beal didn't know it, so we all had the answers as soon as he asked the question, but no clue how we'd come up with them. We learned that if we looked at the ceiling long enough, Mr. Beal seemed to believe we were calculating them in our heads.

"It's not a missing persons thing, yet," the policeman said. "We figure they're goofing around. But their mothers are real worried, and—"

"Were they driving a station wagon?"

"Yes," the policeman said, and he sat up a little higher, looking less self-conscious about his birthmark.

"I saw them," I said, "but we just drove straight back to camp. I haven't seen them since."

"Oh," he said, and I could see his shoulders relax, deflate.

Why was I lying?

Why didn't I tell him that we'd seen the boys,

and plenty? That the redhead and my friend claimed to have seen them sneaking around in the woods in the middle of the night, spying, saying from the other side of the window screen that they were lost in the woods. Why didn't I tell the policeman that they were leaving nasty notes? That they'd been slipping in and out of Pine Ridge Cheerleading Camp since yesterday afternoon when I'd smiled at them, and that we'd passed them on the road, pulled our tops up, or down, and—

That was why.

Whatever those boys were doing, or going to do to us, we'd brought it on ourselves, I knew, and anyone hearing even part of the story—even the first part, that we'd snuck out of camp to avoid doing sit-ups, that we'd wanted to go swimming in Lovers' Lake—would recognize it instantly. And if it came out that we'd flashed our breasts at them? Well, I knew the keys to my Mustang would be hung, permanently, on a hook on the kitchen wall if that story followed me home. But I also knew that anyone hearing that story would believe, whatever happened to us after that, we'd earned it fair and square. I'd learned that by the laws of nature or physics, in self-defense or calculus, long ago on the playground, on the television, in every book I'd ever read that no one ever *believed* a boy, but everyone was always reading between the lines, trying to find out what the girl had done to deserve what she got.

"Can I have your name?" the policeman asked, taking out a little pad of paper and a pencil from his pocket.

"Kristy Sweetland," I said.

"You at the cheerleading camp?"

"Yes," I said.

"How much longer?"

"We leave Sunday."

"If anything else comes up I might have to contact you. Can I have your home phone number and address and your parents' names?"

I told him, but when I gave him the phone number, I reversed the last two numbers. 7487. Our number ended in 7478.

People did it all the time, especially when they were nervous, in a hurry, or talking to a cop.

No one would ever be able to say whether or

not I'd done it on purpose.

Besides, he had my license plate number, I was sure.

Cops can always find you, whether or not you've given them the wrong number.

9

"Can I talk to you?"

Desiree turned around. Her face was flushed. She and the stocky girl and the one with the orange hair had been laughing hard at something. They hadn't seen me coming up behind them. Right away I saw that there was a hickey, deep purple and stippled, like a leech on Desiree's neck. "Oh," she said, turning around. "Sure." The stocky girl narrowed her eyes at me, and I looked away.

"Let's go get some food," Desiree said.

"I need to talk to you alone," I said under my breath, although I knew the two girls heard me. I saw them smirk at each other.

“See you later,” Desiree said to them, and they turned away.

“Did you see that cop?” I asked her when we were halfway to the picnic shelter, holding on to her elbow to stop her.

“What cop?”

“There was a cop. He asked me if I saw those boys.”

“What?”

“He said they disappeared— ”

“The hell they did,” she said.

“I know, I know.”

“What did you tell him?”

“Nothing.” I inhaled. “I told him we’d seen them at the gas station.”

“Why didn’t you tell him those fuckers have been creeping around in the woods spying on us?”

I opened my mouth, but nothing came out.

Desiree pursed her lips and put her hands on her hips. “Forget I asked that,” she said. “It’s because you *like* it.”

“I don’t *like* it. I just thought, I didn’t . . . because of what we *did*.”

“What?”

“You know, flashing them.”

"So?" Desiree said. She looked into my eyes then, as if waiting for an answer.

"So, I—"

"You don't have to tell him that, you idiot."

The way she said "you idiot" was like a quick but painless slap, as if she'd been waiting to say it a long time, had been thinking about it, maybe wanting to say it for years.

"Great," Desiree said. "Well, now if they don't leave us alone, we can't even call the cops, because you *lied*. Now we have to put up with them for the rest of the week, no matter what they do. But," she looked at me with her mouth open, and I could see her tongue pressing against the inside of her cheek, "I guess you like that. I guess that's what this has all been about."

I shook my head.

The tears that burned in my eyes were real, but they felt the same as the others, the ones I'd created out of pink soap in the girls' bathroom a million years ago.

"Let's get some food," Desiree said, walking away from me toward the picnic, the paper plates and enormous stainless steel bowls of potato chips. I walked away from it, from her, in the direction of the barbecue pits and the smell of burning meat, pressing my fingers to my eyes. From somewhere far away, maybe all the way down in the town of St. Sophia, the sound of a bottle rocket pierced the sky.

"Hey," T.J. said when I got to the grill, handing me a paper plate. "Want it raw or burned?" he asked, poking at two hot dogs—one pale pink and perspiring, the other crusted with black. I took a bun out of the plastic bag on the table beside him and said, "Burned."

He stabbed the blackened one and put it on my open bun, pushed it off the prongs with his fingers, and said, "You going with us after the picnic?"

"Where?" I asked.

I saw that he, like Desiree, had a hickey on his neck—although his was redder, rounder, and looked more like a badge than a leech. I couldn't look at him without looking at that hickey, so I looked down at the burned hot dog on my plate instead.

"I stashed a canoe," he gestured with the fork toward some reeds. "We were going to go on the lake. Desiree said you wanted to go too."

I nodded. "Sure, yeah, I guess," I said.

Behind me, the stocky girl said, "Excuse me," and reached around me for a paper plate. "Can you go eat your weenie someplace else?" The orange-haired girl beside her snorted. T.J. stabbed the pink hot dog without asking whether she wanted it or not.

I stepped away from the grill and looked around, but the only place I could see to sit down was at the picnic table next to the other Kristi, who wasn't eating, but staring out into Lovers' Lake with an annoyingly tragic look on her face. She gestured toward me when she saw me glance in her direction, and I went toward her, sighing, although I'd already decided I would not sit down with her, whether or not I had to eat my dinner standing up. "Hi," I said when I got closer, and she stood up fast, as if she'd been waiting for me for hours.

"They're over there," she said, pointing to her left, toward the lake.

"What do you mean?" I asked her.

She was wearing a white tank top, and I could tell she had no bra on under it, because there was a loose fleshiness under there, and I remembered how cool and white her breasts had looked in the backseat of my car. How wide and pink her nipples were. And the memory of it made me want to cover her up, to send her back to her cabin to put something on under her shirt.

She looked terrible.

Her hair was pulled back in a ponytail that looked painful. It was just a fat red rubber band, I could see that, and I winced when I thought of how much it was going to hurt to pull that thing out before she went to bed—or, worse, in the morning, after all the little strands had worked their way around the rubber. She had no makeup on at all, and, without it, I could see that her eyelashes were not black, after all, but pale red, lighter than her hair. Her lips looked chapped. And she smelled like sweat.

"Those boys," she said. "They're watching us from over there."

I shook my head, took a step backward, and looked away from her face, which seemed to be trying to pull my own face into it. I said, "Have you had anything to eat in the last couple days?"

She didn't say anything, just stared off at some spot on the other side of the lake.

There was a small sandy beach that led to a

small group of trees, and behind the trees, a high wall of rock. It must have been where we'd driven the other day, when I'd seen Lovers' Lake through that shivering of white birches, where we'd turned back when the redhead said she had her period, where Desiree had insisted that I make a U-turn.

It would have been *possible* that those boys could be parked up there and, I supposed, with a pair of high-powered binoculars maybe they'd be able to see something through those trees that looked vaguely like some cheerleaders milling around, red, white, and blue in Vet's Park eating hot dogs. But it seemed highly unlikely. I sighed. "Okay," I said. "So what if they are?"

The redhead shrugged, as if she'd learned the gesture from Desiree. "You're right," she said. "So what?"

She sat back down and wouldn't look at me again, so I walked away, down to the water with my hot dog, and stood facing Lovers' Lake with my back to the rest of the picnic.

If they were there, watching, maybe the cop who'd come around asking about them would find them.

Maybe he'd send them home, and they'd get

grounded for the rest of the week.

Was it possible, really, that they'd failed for almost two nights now to go home, to call their mothers, just so they could hang around Pine Ridge Cheerleading Camp watching us?

Were they so bored it seemed like fun to them? Or was it possible that they'd really gotten lost? Had it been that flash of naked flesh that had lured them into the forest? Had they thought it was an invitation? Had it made them crazy?

I thought about the driver, the one with the dark hair and boyishly happy, open smile, how young he'd looked in his plaid shirt—and the other one, with the ratty blond hair. Even in his dark rock band T-shirt, he just looked like a dumb kid. I was pretty sure I'd seen a flash of braces in his mouth when we passed them on the road.

So, was it possible they'd never even dreamed they'd see something like that in St. Sophia—a convertible full of topless cheerleaders passing them on the road? Did they think that there would be more than that in store for them if they could chase us down?

Or could it have been (could it *possibly have been?)* my smile, as Desiree insisted? Had they thought it was a promise? Was it possible the smile, passing between me and the driver of that station wagon—

No.

I thought about the solar system hanging over my bed, its paper light twisting and turning up there . . . *so she can see that the world revolves around the sun, not her.*

There were no boys with binoculars up on that ridge over Lovers' Lake, scanning the park for me, or Desiree, or the other Kristi. The other Kristi was nuts, and so (maybe) was Desiree. Those boys hadn't gone home yet or checked in with their mothers because they'd gotten bored and driven north to some bigger town. Maybe they'd gotten so horny after seeing us that they'd gone looking for some more girls in Mt. Pleasant, and on the way their car had broken down.

In ninth grade, Greg Murray, the school superintendent's son, decided he was in love with me.

At first, it was funny.

Greg was ugly the way some dogs are ugly—so repulsive you can't help but pet them, feel fond of their slimy noses, the disgusting black gums that showed when they growled, the shoved-in features of their faces. Those kinds of dogs, given cute names by their owners (Bing, Princess, Missy) were everywhere and seemed to have been invented specifically to give us something ugly to appreciate.

Greg Murray was tall, with jet-black hair he greased back either with VO5 or his own sweat long after and before greased-back was in style. He had the kind of acne you imagined would feel hot if you put your hand to it. Bubbling, ferocious, angry acne. His pants were always too short. His shoelaces untied. He was neither particularly smart nor stupid in school. If he had any special gifts—humor, kindness, insight—they were never revealed in any of the classes I had with him.

It seemed impossible, by the second marking period of ninth grade, that it could just be a coincidence that Greg Murray was in every one of my classes. "He got his dad to look up what you were taking every hour, and put himself in every class with you," Desiree said.

"Why?" I asked.

"He's obsessed with you."

Okay, I thought. Let him be obsessed. It wasn't bothering me. He never said a word to me, not even when it was just the two of us passing in the hall. Not even when I saw him after school at the library. He never, as far as I could tell, even looked at me.

Then, in the spring, he asked me to go to the

prom with him. He stopped me in the hallway and said it like a challenge, as if he knew I would say no already but had decided to make me say it aloud.

"Will you go to the prom with me?"

There was something infected on his neck. A pimple that must have turned in on itself for a long time, burning just under the surface, until it erupted with pus and blood.

"I can't," I said. "I have a boyfriend."

Everyone knew I was going with Chip Chase. How could he not have known?

"He knew," Desiree said. "He just wanted to make you squirm."

But why?

He walked away fast with a smirk on his face, as if I'd just revealed something shallow and predictable about myself, something he'd suspected for a long time.

Two weeks before prom, Greg Murray rang our front doorbell while I was upstairs taking a shower. He must have walked from his house, which was miles away on the other side of East Grand Rapids, or gotten a ride—someone who dropped him at the end of our driveway, then drove away, leaving him there. My stepfather answered the door.

Greg Murray asked for me, and when my stepfather told him I was unavailable, Greg gave him a little box wrapped in silver paper, asked him to give it to me, and walked away.

My stepfather said he watched Gray Murray walk straight down the middle of the street ("like he was trying to get himself run over") until he couldn't see him anymore.

When I came downstairs with my hair wrapped up in a towel and wearing my robe, my stepfather was standing next to the kitchen table by the little silver box, looking at it suspiciously.

He said, "The ugliest person I've ever seen just dropped this off for you."

"Oh my god," I said. I knew immediately who it was, and I told him.

"Are you going to open it?"

"Should I?"

"I don't know," my stepfather said. We decided to wait until my mother got home from the grocery store, to let her tell me what to do.

She said, "Open it."

"If you'd seen him," my stepfather said, "you wouldn't say that so casually."

We all laughed, but I opened it. Inside, in a little velvet ring box, was the most beautiful antique engagement ring I'd ever seen. The diamond was small, but it was set in what my mother said was "rose gold," intricately inlaid with tiny pearls all around the band. The diamond was so clear it was almost invisible in the brightness of our kitchen, as if a little bit of contained light had been set at the center of that ring.

"Oh my god," my mother and I both said at the same time.

"You're giving that back," my stepfather said.

I called Desiree, who came right over.

"Jesus," she said.

She slipped it onto her ring finger, something I hadn't dared to do—I wasn't sure why.

"I'll take it if you don't want it," she said, holding her left hand away from her face to look at it from a distance.

"My stepfather says I have to give it back," I said.

"Fuck that," Desiree said. "This is yours now."

"No," I said. "If I keep it, he'll—"

"You're right," she said, twisting it off. She made a face. It was on tight, and it hurt to pull it over her knuckle. "Get this out of here," she said. "He's Satan."

"He's not *Satan*," I said.

But that night I had a dream in which I stopped Greg Murray outside homeroom to give him the ring back. He looked at me with his boiling face and said, "You'll burn in hell for this."

"I'm calling his mother," my mother said that night. "This is completely inappropriate behavior for a fifteen year old, giving expensive rings like this. She should know."

"Can you give the ring to her?" I asked. "I don't want to talk to him."

"Yes," my mother said.

I stood at the top of the stairs listening as my mother talked to Mrs. Murray, but all I could hear was my mother saying, "Yes, but. Well. Yes. Okay, I see, but—"

She called me down after she hung up and said, "His mother's insane too. The ring was his great-grandmother's, and it was given to Greg to give to his *fianceé* someday, and when I told Mrs. Murray that you were not going to be Greg's *fianceé,* she said, 'Tell her to keep it anyway. It'll teach him a lesson.'"

I hadn't realized until that moment how much I wanted to keep that ring. That diamond. It was like a little sliver of beauty that had worked its way to my heart through my eye.

"You're not keeping it," she said, reading my mind. "Give it to me," she said with her hand out. "I'm taking it over to their house right now."

The antique engagement ring was gone then, but a florist's van pulled up Saturday afternoon with a dozen red roses in a long white box and a card that said, "Kristy Sweetland. I love you. Greg Murray."

My mother put them in a vase. "We've got a serious problem here," she said.

By Monday morning, everyone in the whole school had heard about the ring and the roses. I'd called Chip, and he'd told his friend Barry. They were going to go beat Greg Murray up, so they called some other guys from the football team, who told their girlfriends, and although they never beat Greg Murray up (they drank Budweiser in Barry's basement and watched television instead, because no one could find anyone old enough to drive), the promise of violence had been crisscrossing the phone lines all over town, and the only person who *hadn't* heard about it by Monday was Greg Murray, who handed me a box, wrapped up in gold paper this time, as he walked by my desk.

I tried to give it back to him as he passed by me again, but he wouldn't put out his hand.

Just as the bell rang, I jumped up from my seat and tossed the box on his desk and hurried out the door.

But I looked back and saw that Greg Murray was gathering up his books and leaving it there.

"You forgot something," Mr. Beal said to him.

"That's Kristy Sweetland's," Greg said, and walked past me out the classroom door.

"Kristy?"

I turned around and picked it up.

Desiree and I opened it up in the girls' room. I'd hoped, I supposed, it would be the same ring again, but it was a different ring this time. An opal, set in a plainer gold band. There were hundreds of colors in that little stone. The surface of it was completely smooth, but just under the surface there seemed to be a little fire full of pale reds and blues and pinks. It had depth the way an eye had depth, implying there was even more where that came from. "Cool," Desiree said.

"It's all yours," I said, and slipped it onto her finger.

In the cafeteria, Desiree showed it off as we waited in line for our trays. Greg Murray stared at me from his usual seat near the door. There was no expression at all on his face.

After school, at home, a letter had come for me in the mail; and my stepfather had set it down on the kitchen table next to the *Seventeen* issue that had come too, and a letter from my pen pal in France (whose pink stationery and foreign handwriting were, after ten years, getting dull). No return address. "Kristy, You know how I feel about you, and believe it or not, I know how you feel about me. You love me. When I look at you, I see God, and that's what you see when you look at me. We will be together for eternity. Yours truly, Greg."

My hands shook. I found my stepfather out back, hosing down the pontoon boat, getting it ready for summer, and showed it to him.

"Oh, Christ. He's delusional," my stepfather said. "I'll go talk to his father, and if that doesn't work we're calling the cops."

But Greg Murray never came back to East Grand Rapids High School. "Oh my God," I said, after he'd been gone a whole week and I saw that his name had been taken off his locker. "I got him kicked out of school for *liking* me."

"Are you serious?" Desiree said. "He didn't just *like* you. And the reason he's not here is either because he's in a mental institution or because his father's the fucking superintendent and had to get his crazy son out of here before it ruined his career. He's probably stalking some girl at Forest Hills as we speak."

Desiree kept the opal, but didn't wear it much. Too tight. I thought about that other ring, the little bit of light pressed into the rose gold, and how, when Greg Murray and I looked at each other, we saw God. For a long time, that was the big joke of the cheerleading squad, but I never saw Greg Murray again, even when, after I got my driver's license and my car, I started driving, every once in a while, past his house.

I was starving.

The outside of my hotdog was burned, but the center was cool and spongy.

The lake looked ominous and inviting at the same time. Slippery Lips had told us that the lake had been made by a meteor. That something hard and big had hit the Earth a million years ago and left this unfathomable crater in its face. Even though the water was black (almost purple) under the darkening sky, it still looked clean. A lake that deep, I thought, probably stayed pretty pure. The bad stuff sank to the bottom and stayed there. The top was refreshed every couple of weeks with rain.

Right?

I was thirsty, but more than that I was ravenous and wanted to finish eating my hot dog before going back up to the picnic shelter to fish a can of soda out of the cooler. I looked behind me and saw that most of the other cheerleaders, and all of the counselors, were looking in the direction of T.J., who had now stepped away from the barbecue pit and was striking matches over what looked like the kind of cardboard tube that hid at the center a roll of paper towels. It must have been some kind of firecracker instead, because they all jumped back at the same time as it ripped into the sky and exploded with a loud *zzzz-ap*. In the flash of it I saw Desiree in her red halter top and shorts, staring straight into the sky, although most of the others had cringed and covered their faces.

Standing in the grass near the statue of the soldier were a few other cheerleaders twirling sparklers, which spit and hissed little darts around their heads, and fizzled out at their feet. The sun had all but set, just a deep pink glow over the other end of Lovers' Lake, and it lit up the pine trees like arrows. Only the other Kristi was looking in my direction, and she seemed to be gazing far across the lake, not noticing me at all, looking for those boys. So I stepped up to the edge of the water, and although I'd been warned a million times not to, I knelt down and cupped my right hand under the surface of it and drank from it—the coolest and freshest water I'd ever tasted, or would ever taste again. I stood up just as the first blast exploded from the other side of the lake, and looked.

It was like a huge, slippery rose in the sky, shimmering before being ripped into a million pieces, being turned into burning tears and earrings, and drifting down from the darkness onto the surface of the lake, where it sizzled and writhed for a moment, then disappeared.

From the other side of the lake where the Kiwanis Club of St. Sophia must have been producing the display, we heard *oooohs* and *aaahs.* These exhalations floated as a single note through the trees, and for just a moment it seemed to me that this sound of awe was coming *from* the trees, as if the trees had finally learned how to sing, and that this was what they sang, this airy vowel sound, in response to the burning drizzle descending on their branches. The note was abruptly snuffed, though, by another explosion, followed by a white flash of light, and then several slithering snakes—

red, white, and blue—that screamed, chased their own tails, then turned to smoke in midair and were gone.

I sat down in the sandy grass and leaned back, and there was another—a white thing, like a peony, that blew up before it even formed, and then dissolved in a luminous mist that blew sideways over Lovers' Lake, over the national forest. This was followed by one detonated flower after another—the whole celestial garden getting blown to bits while I watched. It seemed to go on forever, each explosion followed by that chorus of *ooooh-aaaah*, until finally there was a last hurrah of five or six blasts right on top of one another, a dozen little stars shot out of the sky followed by one huge shrieking, screaming, whistling thing that flashed over and over overhead as if the world were coming to an end. From the other side of the lake I could hear cheers and a trumpet playing "The Star-Spangled Banner." I felt, by then, as if I'd been on my back at the edge of Lovers' Lake staring up at the show in the sky for my whole life, but also that it had begun and ended in an instant.

"Time to go!" Slippery Lips called out. I started to stand up, but someone touched my shoulder.

Desiree. She and T.J. were right behind me. He was lying down on a beach towel, and she was sitting up beside me. Had they been there the whole time?

"Not us," she said. "We're going out there."

I could see her only dimly in the light of the moon, but I knew she was nodding toward Lovers' Lake. "You coming with us?" T.J. asked. He was inviting me.

I said, "Okay."

"Just lay low for a few minutes then," Desiree said, "until everybody's cleared out. They can't see us down here. Maybe they won't know we stayed behind."

I said nothing, but lay back down and turned my face back to the sky—which, except for just a haze of moonlight coming up from some spot I couldn't locate (as if the moon had slipped out of space into the forest somewhere and gotten lost in it)—was nothing but darkness and stars. And now that the fireworks were over, those stars seemed to be gathering themselves together to shine, blinking on one by one, as if someone were going around up there turning on lights. They were blurred, so many of them they appeared to be in motion, as if they were the million ghosts of the moths I'd killed with my car, frothing around up there, making light out of the darkness.

From the parking lot, I could hear van and car doors slamming and some cheerleader singing "The Star-Spangled Banner" in a mocking falsetto. And someone else, maybe Slippery Lips, giving instructions about watching your step when you got into the van.

Directly behind me I could hear Desiree and the lifeguard doing what I hoped was just making out—rhythmic breathing, the sound of mouths. The painful and pleasurable little exhalations, the quick inhalations. I tried not to listen, but it was impossible not to hear them.

I'd never let Chip give me a hickey, although he'd suggested it once. I wouldn't let him because I knew why he'd wanted to, so his friends on the football team would see it. "My mother will kill me," I told him, pushing his face away from my neck. Once or twice he'd tried to put his hand up my cheerleading skirt or down my shorts, but when I'd nudged it off, he'd given up quickly and without complaint. A few times when my parents were out of town, he'd rested all of his weight on my body on the couch in the living room, and feeling his heart beating over mine made it speed up, but then the weight had become uncomfortable. When I rolled him off of me, he seemed relieved. The subject of having sex never came up, and whatever that uncontrollable urge was that came over other teenage couples and landed them at Planned Parenthood taking pregnancy tests and making appointments for abortions never happened to us.

At any point, either one of us seemed just as happy to get up from the couch and get some chips and Sprite as anything else we might have done.

Lying there, watching the stars beat their wings in the darkness, hearing the two of them behind me, I knew it would be different with T.J. I could imagine that shark's tooth pressing into my neck, and I heard Desiree gasp with a kind of pleasure I knew I'd never had.

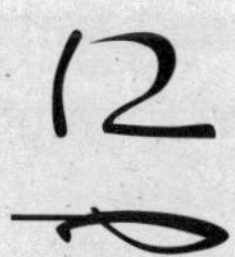

T.J. took his shoes off and waded into the lake to pull the canoe onto the sand. It made a gasping sound as he dragged it through the reeds and into the shallow water.

"Here," he said, holding out his hand.

My eyes had adjusted to the darkness, and the moon had risen completely over the tops of the trees, so I could see him standing there shirtless with his arm stretched out, guiding me from the sand to the boat. I'd left my own shoes on a picnic table beside his and Desiree's, and with T.J.'s warm, smooth hand in mine, the sand felt surprisingly cold on my feet. The canoe rocked when I stepped in, but T.J. steadied it with his knee. "There's a flashlight under that seat," he said. "Grab it before it gets wet."

After I sat down, I picked up the flashlight, feeling the solid weight of it in my hands, but I didn't turn it on.

Desiree climbed in next, and when she sat down beside me I could feel the tense flesh and muscle of her arm next to mine before she scooted over and grabbed a paddle.

"This might be hard to do with two people back here," she said. "Maybe you can sit behind me, on the bottom of the boat."

I did. In the corner, on the floor of the boat where I slid down, there was a bit of cool water, but I sat in it anyway. If we were going to go swimming, we were going to get wet one way or another.

T.J. pulled the boat farther into the lake, and then he slipped gracefully into the canoe. The weight of it shifted when he did, and I had to hold on to both sides, realizing even as I did it that it would do me no good, that if the boat tipped over what I was holding on to was the unsteadiness of the boat itself.

T.J. put a paddle in the water then and pushed us off from shore."You girls okay?" he asked when we were moving smoothly, like a soft and heavy arrow, over the water. "You're being awfully quiet."

He picked up the flashlight and shone it on us, and the white beam was so bright and painful, I covered my eyes.

Desiree said, "I'm fine."

"Me too," I said, looking up when he switched off the flashlight.

"You sure you're brave enough to do this?" T.J. asked, teasing. "It's supposed to be bottomless, you know."

"And full of leeches," Desiree said.

I laughed at the reference to Little Miss Frigid, but it reminded me of what she'd told me. I said, "The redhead told me those hicks from the station wagon are over there"—I pointed to the side of the lake where the ridge was—"watching us."

"What?" Desiree said, and turned to look at me. In the moonlight, her hair looked as if it were made of water.

"She claims that they—"

"Those assholes," Desiree said, and turned back around. Her paddle made a clumsy slur against the surface of the water, and the canoe moved to the right.

"Come on, Desiree," I said. "There's no way. And even if there *was* some way before, they can't be watching us now anyway. It's pitch-black. Besides, she's nuts. She has no way of knowing where those guys are. She's just paranoid."

"Well, we can check it out easy enough," T.J. said. "Maybe that's where we should go. We can't just hop into the lake and swim, anyway. We've got to be docked. I don't feel like dragging the lake for your bodies in the morning."

"Oh," Desiree said, whining a little. "I wanted to just hop into the middle." I couldn't tell whether or not she was serious, but T.J. laughed.

"Yeah," he said, "but you're crazy," and then she laughed too, and the intimacy of it started up a strange heartbeat in my throat. I had to swallow hard to get it to go away.

The farther into the center of the lake we got, the more light there seemed to be on the water—more than in the sky. The moon was unraveling on the surface of it, and the stars too seemed to be shining up from the bottom of Lovers' Lake rather than down onto it from the sky. As T.J. and Desiree paddled, they broke up the light on the surface of the water, but there appeared to be so little resistance that the lake seemed barely there, as if we were rowing through air, or time, or nothing at all.

On Desiree's hair, a weird halo of moonlight glowed. It slipped down to rest around her neck when she stopped paddling, and then rose and hovered over her again when she started paddling again. It felt to me that what I was staring into was the endlessness of it, the bottomlessness, but, when the canoe ran aground with a muffled sound, coming to an abrupt stop in sand, I realized that we'd been near the shore all along, that we'd never drifted into the deep middle of Lovers' Lake at all.

When T.J. jumped out to pull the canoe onto the sand, I looked back in the direction I thought we'd come from. The moon had reversed itself: it was behind us now, lying flat and white as an empty dinner plate in the lake. And Desiree's halo of moonlight had turned into a lopsided tiara. When she raked her hand through her hair stepping out of the boat, it slipped off into the water.

"Hey!" T.J. shouted to the ridge that rose up in front of us, sandwiching us between itself and the lake. "You fuckers want something to look at?!"

Far above us, I saw what looked like headlights driving on what might have been the road over us—two distant white eyes traveling through the darkness. Although it was right in front of me,

I couldn't really see that steep bank, but I was sure it was the one I'd looked down on from the other side, the day before, driving near the edge of it in my Mustang, feeling dizzily afraid of crashing over it. From this perspective it didn't feel dangerous. It felt almost comforting, as if we were being cradled and protected by it, as if it were a buffer between us and the rest of the world, and I wondered if this was what it had felt like to be a baby in a bassinet, or held in a father's arms.

In the Midwest, it was rare to see a cliff like this. Hills, mountains, canyons—all those land formations that reminded you there'd once been an ice age, or meteors, that you were living on the face of something enormous, eternal, and indifferent—we didn't have those. So this ravine (which, in the dark, looked to be really not much more than a darkness erected inside another darkness) was interesting to me.

"Hey!" T.J. shouted at it again. "You hicks wanna see some chicks? Huh?"

But there was no response at all, not even an echo. T.J.'s words were just absorbed by the trees and the enormous wall of earth out of which they grew.

"Well," he said, more quietly, to us, "I guess we don't have company after all. Want to go for a swim?"

Without answering him Desiree started untying her halter top.

I stepped out of the canoe for the first time and felt the solid ground beneath me. The sand here was the same temperature as my body, and it felt warm on my bare feet after the cold floor of the canoe.

About eight feet away, T.J. had taken off his shorts and was standing in the moonlight in his underwear, which shone whitely in the darkness. When he pulled those off too, tossing them behind him in the reedy sand, it looked as if he were still wearing them because of the tan of his legs and torso against the pale flesh kept hidden from the sun by his bathing suit.

I pulled my tube top over my head. In the darkness, I didn't feel naked. I felt as if I were changing clothes, not taking them off.

A sweet smell drifted through the birches on the ridge (a smell like old roses—half flowers, half meat), and the sand felt silty and stiff, like cornstarch or talcum powder. I slipped out of my shorts and underwear and turned around to face the lake.

Desiree and T.J. were already up to their shoulders, facing each other, bobbing. A straight line of moonlight traveled across the water like a path between them, dividing them from one other, even though they were only inches from each other's bodies. "Hey, Slowpoke!" Desiree called out. "The water's perfect."

Perfect for what, I wondered, stepping into it, walking in up to my thighs. It wasn't cold, but the shock of it on my body raised goose bumps all over my flesh anyway, stiffened my nipples, made me bare my teeth.

"You get used to it fast," T.J. said reassuringly. He was looking at me. I looked down at myself. I was silver, like a shadow or a veil, and insubstantial looking, even to myself.

I waded farther in.

There were pebbles on the bottom.

Slimy pebbles.

I imagined them green with algae under my feet.

Then, something fluttered past my ankle. It might have been seaweed, or a minnow, or something else entirely. I didn't know, but I kept walking until I was up to my waist, holding my arms over my head. Then suddenly the sand and the pebbles disappeared beneath my feet and I was simply walking on nothing, floating and sinking at the same time. I thrashed a bit and saw the surface of the water shatter into little sections of light and darkness. T.J. said, "Whoa. You gotta tread," and I felt his hands on my waist, holding me up in the water, and the motion of his legs treading near mine.

"Good thing we've got a lifeguard with us," Desiree said. She laughed and flipped smoothly onto her back, floating. Her breasts seemed to drift by themselves on the water, like pale globes.

So, we swam like that for a long time. T.J. dove under us now and then, and I could feel him pass beneath my body, a current made out of flesh. I watched the membrane of the water, waiting to see where he would surface, and when he broke back up for a breath it was a smooth ascent, hardly a ripple, a soft incision in the body of the lake.

It was easy, after my initial thrashing, to stay afloat. This didn't require swimming, which I was good at. This was something else. Abandonment. Amnesia. This drifting. I moved my legs and arms around me in slow motion, occasionally lying back and looking up at the sky, feeling the depths below me as vividly as the heights above me. They felt like the same thing to me. It felt as if I could have slipped just as easily, forever, into either direction if some invisible force weren't keeping me where I was.

For a long time, we floated around one another in silence before T.J. said, "We're getting too far away from the shore. Time to swim in."

Desiree and I followed him, the two of us doing the breast stroke side by side. As we got closer to the shore, the temperature of the water changed, warming only a little, but enough that I could feel there was something under us again, a bottom to the darkness, an end to the unfathomable.

T.J. was the first to get to the little beach, and he stood up, and it seemed strange for just a moment to remember that he had legs, that, like us, he could walk as well as swim.

"I'll get the towels," he said and sprinted over to the canoe.

Desiree crawled onto the shore then and lay on the sand looking up at the sky. Her eyes filled with moon, as if the light of it were some kind of molten silver, as if her eyes were bottomless holes, like Lovers' Lake, taking it in. I stood over her—cool, but not shivering—and looked down into the strange illusion of her eyes.

When T.J. brought the towels over, he tossed one down to her and snapped the other one into the air over my shoulders and around them, and pulled me to him.

The feeling of flesh rushing suddenly against mine was like the water—except for his erection, which pressed hard into my stomach. He put his mouth on my neck, and then he lay me backward onto the sand, beside Desiree—and even though I tried to open my eyes, I couldn't, and suddenly my whole body was throbbing, like a ripple. But instead of beginning somewhere and traveling across the water, it began and ended everywhere at once.

I woke to silence when the sun came up. They were truly dead, it seemed—the cicadas had died just when I'd learned to expect to hear them in the mornings. T.J. was lying on his back beside me, and Desiree had her head on his chest, her face completely covered by her hair, her shoulders and chest covered with his arm and her Malibu Barbie beach towel. Her legs were bare and sandy, tangled with his. I'd woken only a few inches away from them, on my side, with my head resting in the crook of my elbow and another towel, a white one, over me like a blanket, as if someone had placed it on me carefully, then tucked me in.

I leaned back on my elbows and looked out over the water.

On the other side, the sun was beginning to bleed pinkly through the pine trees, and the pastel of it made Lovers' Lake seem even blacker than it had in the night.

I wasn't cold. The sand was warm from my body, and the air was fresh but not cool. It would be a hot day, I thought, if it was starting out this warm already. It would have been a day that would have made cicadas scream like crazy—except that they were gone already, after all of that, and it would be seventeen years before they'd be back.

I needed to pee.

And I knew we had to get back to camp.

If someone hadn't already noticed that we'd never come back from the picnic, they would soon, and God only knew what would happen then. They'd call our parents, for sure. They might send out rangers and helicopters and bloodhounds for all I knew.

I had to wake up T.J. and Desiree, but I felt suddenly shy. I wanted to be dressed and to have peed already in the reeds before I woke them. Holding the towel over my breasts, I made my way across the sand and over the pebbles until I was far enough away that I wasn't worried they would hear me.

I peed, the heat and the familiar smell of it rose up from the sand, and then I stood up, wiped myself with a corner of the towel and turned around, looking for wherever it was I had tossed my clothes the night before, scanning the strip of beach near the place where the canoe was tied to a tree stump for a glimpse of the red, white, and blue.

Then I heard something behind me.

A low, slow creaking, like a heavy door on rusty hinges being pushed open. Or a boulder at the edge of a cliff, about to go over. I turned fast in the direction of the sound, and what I saw, at first, simply confused me.

It was impossible, I thought, looking at it.

No one could have *driven* here.

The ridge between *here* and the road was forty feet high, and no one could have come from the other direction, because the only thing to drive on was water.

No.

Nor could a rusty station wagon have been flown down to this spot from the sky. No matter what those boys had done to try to spy on us, there was no way a station wagon could be at the bottom of that ridge, twenty feet away from me, parked in a tangle of birch trees.

What I saw, I thought, couldn't be what I was seeing.

It was something else.

It was a piece of junk.

It was something someone had pushed off the road and down into this ravine, maybe hoping it would roll right into the lake and be gone forever—a piece of machinery, or a car that had broken down in the driveway and would cost more to tow away than it was worth.

I stepped toward it.

Because the leaves of the birch trees obscured the rusty metal, I couldn't tell if I was approaching from the back or from the front, but as I continued in the direction of it, I heard that sound again—the sound of something traveling toward me in such slow increments it was as if time had stopped. As if time had been replaced by gravity, and whatever was behind the trees, was being nudged forward only because the earth was turning, so slowly that the turning was imperceptible.

There were those trees between us.

White trunked, peeling in long bandages, like mummies.

Some of them were only saplings. Their trunks were thin as branches, and I pushed them out of the way. My feet hurt from climbing over the branches and the stones, but I didn't stop. I was being pulled toward it as if by invisible ropes, as if it were singing something to me that I needed to hear, and, even after I realized what it was and saw what I thought I saw, I could not stop wanting to hear it, I could not stop walking toward it:

Crumpled roof, pieces of steel and chrome scattered around it, a boy in a plaid shirt slumped where he must have tried to crawl out the window of his car—before he couldn't.

The windshield was a blizzard of broken glass, and the other boy (whose orange cap had come to rest on the hood of the car)—that boy's face had broken through it, covered in blood, alive with flies, arms spread out in front of him as if he were an angel with wings, as if he'd tried to fly through something bright on his way to something even brighter and had almost made it, but had gotten caught instead between one brilliant place and the next. There was a look of amazement on his face. I screamed.

And screamed.

I kept screaming, and my screams woke T.J., who, with the Barbie towel wrapped around his waist and the flashlight in his hand (although it was pure daybreak now, and everything was illuminated by sun) and with Desiree by his side (who ran up behind me, naked, her hair a golden mess around her head), put a hand over my mouth to stop me from screaming and said, "What the—"

I shrugged him away and whirled around and shouted at Desiree, "It's *them! It's them.* They haven't been *following* us. We *killed* them."

She backed away, shaking her head.

"What?" she said, as if she really hadn't heard me, putting a hand to her mouth, taking it away. "What?"

"We were *right here*," I said, pointing to the edge of the cliff. "We flashed them *right here,* and they tried to turn around, and they couldn't, and they—"

She was staring over my shoulder, transfixed.

She stared for a long time, then said, "But I saw them. At camp. And their car—"

"No, you didn't," I said, pounding the fist of one hand into the palm of the other. "It wasn't them. I *told* you it wasn't them. *This* is them."

Desiree's eyes grew even wider, and from where I stood looking into them, I thought I could see the accident reflected there, but when I looked more closely I saw that what she was looking at was T.J.

"What are you doing?" she asked, and I turned to see him walking slowly toward it, stepping up to the car door, reaching for the door handle, every muscle in his back tensed, the Barbie beach towel still around his waist. He had almost gotten to it, almost reached out and touched it, when he staggered backward, shouting, "Oh fuck! Oh fuck!" stumbling to the ground, getting up again. "Oh fuck!" he shouted, sobbing now. "The fucking driver's not dead."

Desiree (who hadn't even gotten close enough to see that there was a driver in there at all or that he was slumped over the steering wheel and the door of his car at the same time) screamed and ran toward Lovers' Lake, grabbing her clothes off the ground as she ran, still screaming and running, running toward the canoe now, stumbling as she pulled her shorts up, running at the same time she was tying her halter top behind her neck.

T.J. turned around and looked at me, and his

face was blank. He said, just loud enough for me to hear over his sob, "He's still breathing," and then he staggered past me and bent over, vomiting into the sand.

I went to T.J. "Give me the flashlight," I said.

15

No one had even noticed that we were gone. All the other cheerleaders were in the dining hall having breakfast when Desiree and I ran down from the parking lot to the girls' room, washed our hands and brushed our hair, stuffed our clothes into the trash can, and went back to our cabins wrapped in towels.

At pep, I thought Slippery Lips was looking at me strangely, but when I met her eyes and smiled, she smiled back.

It was a warm morning, and the pregnant pep coach was wearing a bathing suit top and drawstring shorts, and the whole huge mound of her stomach was shining in the sun.

It was unreal.

I could hardly stand to look at it, and, at the same time, I felt giddy looking at it.

I felt as if I might stand up and start screaming, or laughing, or cheering at the top of my lungs if I didn't keep the fingernails of one hand digging into the palm of the other. When I couldn't stand the pain of it anymore, I switched hands.

She was calm that morning, the pep coach, speaking to us quietly, not needing to shout over the sound of cicadas anymore. She was telling us a few things for our own good, but she didn't need to use a megaphone to do it.

"Girls," she said. "Cheerleading is public relations. Not only do you need to get along with your squadmates, you have to show the team, the officials, the crowd, and the community that you have spirit, that you are an 'I'll help out' kind of girl.

"You can't be a quitter.

"You need to be the kind of girl who's charming without being overbearing, the kind of girl who makes friends easily, who always has a pleasant smile, even when you're in a bad mood. The main goal of a cheerleader is to be a *perfect girl*."

Desiree had dropped down behind the bleachers before the pep coach even started her speech, and left with the stocky girl and the other one, the one with orange hair.

For the last few days of camp, she would be with them all the time without me. On the drive back to East Grand Rapids, mostly we would not speak, and, back at school, we would be friendly when we saw each other in the halls, but Desiree would quit the squad, and we'd never be alone together again.

"Your friend's gained a lot of weight since she quit cheerleading," Margo would say to me one day after practice, and I'd say, "Who?"

"Desiree," she'd say.

And I'd say, "Oh, I didn't know," and it would be the truth. Whenever I would pass Desiree in the hallway I'd never let my eyes rest on her long enough to notice anything.

The pep coach continued:

"The sky's the limit for a girl with the energy and commitment it takes to always look her best, to do her best, *be* her best," she said. There were a few crows flying around from one pine tree behind her to another, but they made no noise.

After morning chores, T.J. went back to his cabin, but then the camp director announced to us that night at dinner that he'd gotten sick, gone home, that T.J. had a fever, maybe even mono, that he wouldn't be back, but that we should feel free, as a group, to make a card, and he would send it to T.J.'s parents' house.

The other Kristi rolled over on her cot beside me that night and said, "They're not coming back." I knew what she meant. I said nothing. But the next day when she sat down across me at breakfast with two pancakes on her plate, before she'd even finished saying, "Hi," I'd said, "How did you know?"

She cut into the edge of one of her pancakes with the side of her fork.

"How did I know what?" she asked.

"About the boys," I said impatiently. "How did you know where they were?"

She put the flimsy fork down on the rim of her plate and said, "I saw it. Remember? I was in the backseat. I turned around, and I saw it."

"You saw them go over the fucking ridge?" I whispered in a hiss, leaning across the table toward her. "And you didn't say anything?"

She put a bite of the pancake into her mouth and said, "There was nothing to say."

"Okay," I said, pushing myself away from the table. "Okay, so there was nothing to say. Then why did you *lie*?"

"What do you mean?"

"Why did you say you'd seen them in the woods? Why did you say you talked to them through the fucking window screen?"

"I didn't lie," she said, shaking her head. "I did see them. And I did talk to them." She shrugged. It was Desiree's shrug. She said, "They were lost." She took a sip of apple juice from her glass, then looked up at me blankly. "Aren't you going to eat anything?" she asked. I couldn't tell if she was being sarcastic, but I looked down at my plate. On it I had only a piece of cantaloupe, sliced into a pale orange smile, and it smelled spoiled.

"Fuck you," I said, looking back up at her. What I'd said hadn't registered on her face at all, and although she was being completely quiet, I said, "Shut *up*. What the hell is this all about? Why did you tell me, that night, that something *terrible* was going to happen if you knew it already *had*?"

"That wasn't it," she said. "I meant that something terrible was going to happen to *you*." She picked up her fork then and pointed it at me, her head cocked to one side.

I stood up fast from the table, my heart pounding, walked away without taking my plate, and never spoke to her again.

On the last day, her father would pick her up in a long tan car and, as he drove her away, she would wave at me, but I wouldn't wave back.

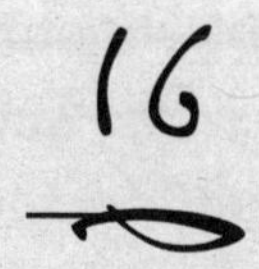

What was, I would wonder (just as I'm sure she had wanted me to wonder), the terrible thing—the terrible thing that would happen or had already happened?

This is what happened:

I walked with the flashlight back to the station wagon, opened the driver's side door, and saw that every part of him was broken, smashed, strung with blood, that there were parts of him that should have been inside him, outside of him, parts of him that had been turned around, crushed, that everything about the boy I'd smiled at, the one in the plaid shirt who'd smiled back, was over, wrecked, a ruin. The boy who had been out driving around in his rusty car, looking for girls, stunned to find a Mustang full of cheerleaders with their tops off on a summer day in a small town on the edge of the national forest, and who'd tried to turn around to follow them (probably hooting with his buddy, stupidly thinking that the shoulder would hold them if he turned around fast enough)—that boy was gone. Utterly gone.

And then he breathed.

Out.

A terrible drowning snore that went on and on until it finally stopped—and before he could draw another breath, a sound I knew I couldn't stand to hear, I brought the flashlight down with all the strength I had on the back of his head.

And then, again.

And I raised it once more, but then realized I wouldn't be needing it anymore, that he would not be breathing again.

It was already facing the lake, that station wagon. And, between where it was and where it was going, it was all downhill. I'd already heard the low groan of gravity, and the wheels were intact—it was already on its way. When they had gone over the ridge, the station wagon must have landed hard on the roof, and then been tossed on its side before sliding smoothly upright again, and now all I needed to do was to reach over the dead boy, shift it into neutral, and, as T.J., sobbing, pushed from behind, steer it easily over the sand, through the reeds, and into Lovers' Lake, where, without even a whisper, it would sink and disappear forever.

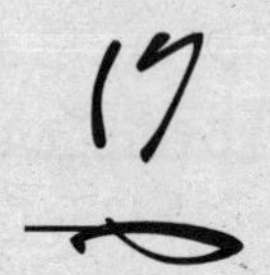

The cheerleaders listened to their counselor, whose face was a mass of flames in the light of the campfire.

"So," she said, "they never found the boys."

"And they never found the station wagon, either?" one girl asked, and another, sitting next to her, elbowed her playfully and said, "It's a *story,* airhead."

"No," the counselor said, "it's *true.* They call that ridge Boy Heaven for a *reason.* And every year or two somebody who's never even been around here before and never heard this story gets lost in the woods. They'll later tell someone that a grungy guy with an orange cap came along and led them out. He doesn't speak. He just motions for them to follow him until they get back to a road, and then he just vanishes when they try to thank him."

"How come they never found the car?"

"Because it's the deepest lake in the state," the counselor said. "They say it's bottomless, but that's just because the bottom is like quicksand. Nothing that sinks in there ever comes back out of that lake."

"What happened to Desiree and the Kristies?"

The counselor looked around at the girls, and inhaled. "Well," she said, "At first everything was fine. The one with the red convertible went back to her high school. She was Homecoming Queen. She got into a good college. She got married to a doctor, and they moved to Chicago. She had a baby boy.

"But one summer night not too long ago, when they were driving home from a weekend up at their cottage, some teenage boys, just as a prank, dangled a scarecrow they'd stolen from a farmer's field down off the overpass, onto the freeway.

"She was driving, and when she saw it, she must have thought it was a person because she swerved to miss it, and the car flipped off the road.

"The baby and the husband were thrown

onto the grass. Not even scratched.

"But she was trapped behind the steering wheel. The car burst into flames. And even after the fire trucks got there, they couldn't get close enough to help her.

"They say that from inside the car they could hear her screaming for help, but when no help came, at the very end, she started to sing."

"Holy shit."

Another silence.

"Well, what about the other ones?" someone asked.

"No one knows for sure, but they say it wasn't good. One got killed during an earthquake in South America. Another one's in a mental institution. She's always telling the people who work there that boys are following her through the hallways, staring at her through the windows, but of course no one believes her."

Something screeched, as if on cue, in the dark trees behind them, and the campfire surged with light as a thin page from a magazine caught fire at the center, and then it sank back down.

"What happened to the boys' mothers?"

"The cops called, told them they thought they

found where the car went off the road. But when they never found the car or the bodies they say that at least one of the mothers killed herself and the other wandered off into the woods, where she's still looking for her son.

"Sometimes cheerleaders say they've seen her watching them from the woods and that you can hear her sobbing in the forest on quiet nights, calling her son's name. She still blames the cheerleaders from Pine Ridge. When something goes wrong here—you know, those girls who drowned swimming at night, or that one a few years ago who went up on the roof of the dining hall to sunbathe and fell off and broke her neck—they say it's *her.*

"Maybe," the counselor continued, quietly, "she's watching us now."

There was laughter, but it was thin and nervous. "Bullshit," someone said.

"Hey," the counselor said, "I just said it was a true story, I didn't say you had to believe it."

Acknowledgments

I'd like to thank Bill Abernethy, Lisa Bankoff, Tara Weikum, and Tina Dubois Wexler for the patience, support, and brilliant advice that made this book possible. And Jack Abernethy, for telling me a new story every day.